Penguin Books

The Ruba'iyat of Omar Khayyam

TRANSLATED BY PETER AVERY AND JOHN HEATH-STUBBS

PENGUIN BOOKS

PENGUIN BOOKS

Published by the Penguin Group
Penguin Books Ltd, 27 Wrights Lane, London W8 5TZ, England
Penguin Books USA Inc., 375 Hudson Street, New York, New York 10014, USA
Penguin Books Australia Ltd, Ringwood, Victoria, Australia
Penguin Books Canada Ltd, 10 Alcorn Avenue, Toronto, Ontario, Canada M4V 3B2
Penguin Books (NZ) Ltd, 182–190 Wairau Road, Auckland 10, New Zealand

Penguin Books Ltd, Registered Offices: Harmondsworth, Middlesex, England

First published by Allen Lane 1979
Published in Penguin Books 1981
10

Translation copyright © Peter Avery and John Heath-Stubbs, 1979
All rights reserved

Printed in China
Set in Palatino

Introduction   7
Note on the Translations   32

Translations of the Ruba'iyat
From a selection made by Sadiq Hedayat   37
From a selection made by
Muhammad 'Ali Furughi and Qasim Ghani   86

Appendix 1: Omar Khayyam,
the Assassins and the Three Schoolfellows   115
Appendix 2: Khayyam and Some Nineteenth-century 'Sufis'
in Kabul   120
Appendix 3: Background to the Illustrations   122

List of Illustrations   126
Bibliography   128

The Ruba'i

The ruba'i, pronounced *rubā'ī*, plural *rubā'īyāt*, is a two-lined stanza of Persian poetry, each line of which is divided into two hemistichs making up four altogether, hence the name *ruba'i*, an Arabic word meaning 'foursome'. The Persians also called this verse form *taraneh*, 'snatch', or, for a form very close to it, *dobaiti*, 'two-liner'. The first, second and last of the four hemistichs must rhyme. The third need not rhyme with the other three, a point Fitzgerald noticed, so that he made the first, second and fourth lines of his quatrains rhyme:

> Dreaming when Dawn's Left Hand was in the *sky*
> I heard a Voice within the Tavern *cry*,
> 'Awake my little ones, and fill the Cup
> Before Life's Liquor in its Cup be *dry*'.

This escape from a monorhymed pattern, coupled with the ruba'i's shortness, no doubt partly accounted for its great popularity in north-east Persia in the eleventh and twelfth centuries, the period of Khayyam and of many famous ruba'is which have survived. Persian poets had been following Arabic models in which long, monorhymed poems predominated. The rise of the ruba'i coincided with revulsion from lengthy and highly artificial panegyrics and narrative poems in a single rhyme. The ruba'i demanded less from poets who had been constrained to make numerous lines end in the same rhyming letter. It was on a far less extended scale than the poems in which court poets were expected to display their ingenuity. Its force lay in the capacity to make a short and telling statement. An epigrammatic stanza, the ruba'i generally consists of a descriptive or reflective opening, the moral of which is clinched in the last line; as the seventeenth-century Persian poet Sa'ib said, 'In the ruba'i the last line thrusts the finger nail into the heart.'

Such a form enabled witty and intelligent people to strike off easily remembered expressions of feeling or opinion, regardless of the conventions of the poetry of courts and flattery. Each ruba'i is a separate entity, standing by itself, not part of a sequence. Fitzgerald knew this but preferred to present his selection 'strung together into something of an Eclogue'. In original Persian collections of ruba'is the poems are arranged in alphabetical order according to the last letter of the rhyme. As Fitzgerald said, since they represent no connected thought or narrative, thus collected the stanzas make 'a strange Farrago of Grave and Gay'.[1]

A thirteenth-century manual of Persian poetics emphasizes how popular the ruba'i was, eagerly taken up by both 'the educated and the uneducated, the pure and the debauched, to be used for purposes good and bad'. The same manual claims that the ruba'i is a purely Persian innovation. It tells a legend about its discovery. One of the 'early poets of Persia, I think it was Rudaki, but God knows best', is described as walking about the city of Ghazna – Ghazni in present-day Afghanistan – on a public holiday. He saw some boys playing marbles with walnuts, and one of them said, *'Ghalatan ghalatan hami ravad ta bun-i-ku'* ('Rolling, rolling it is running to the end of the lane'). Struck by this line, he took it as the basis for the ruba'i metres, many variants of which were derived from the metre of the boy's lively, action-filled 'verse'.[2]

It is probable that the ruba'i was of older origin than this legend suggests. Alessandro Bausani in the *Storia della letteratura persiana* (Milan, 1960) makes an extremely plausible case for a Turco–Central Asian origin of the quatrain, a form comparable with Chinese four-line stanzas of the T'ang period between the seventh and ninth centuries, as well as with the Japanese *haiku* and Malaysian *pantum*. There is evidence for the existence in north-eastern Persia in the eleventh century of popular poetry in Turkish,

1. Edward Fitzgerald's Introduction to the *Ruba'iyat of Omar Khayyam*, p.XIII in the first (1859) edition. See A. J. Arberry, *The Romance of the Rubaiyat*, London, 1959, p.161. Cf. E. G. Browne, *Literary History of Persia*, Vol. II, Cambridge, 1956, p.35 and p.259.

2. Shamsu'd-Din Muhammad ibn Qais ar-Razi, *Al-Mu'jam fi ma'ayir ash'ar al-Ajam* ('Enlightening Book on the Touchstones of Persian Poetry'), Leyden and London, 1909, pp.88–91. This treatise on Persian poetics was completed in about A.D. 1233. The author had found asylum in the southern city of Shiraz after escaping from the Mongol invasion of northern Persia led by Chinghiz Khan and his sons. Shamsu'd-Din had begun his work on poetics in Marv in Khurasan as early as 1217.

current among Turkish soldiers descended from Central Asian tribal ancestors. The *ruba'i* as we know it is, however, a purely Persian phenomenon, developed out of what was no doubt an older popular form, quite possibly in a Central Asian Turkic dialect, but in Persian transformed into a part of recorded literature, crystallized in a classical mould with its own distinctive rules and limitations. As Bausani suggests, Shamsu'd-Din Muhammad-i-Qais's legend of the ruba'i's 'discovery' may be taken to mark this transformation, the quatrain's establishment as part of the Persian literary tradition. Such a story of how the ruba'i came to be recognized perhaps arose out of its wide currency in the eleventh and twelfth centuries, when people would want to establish an origin for it. By bringing in the name of Rudaki even casually, the author of the manual did two things: he conferred on a popular verse-form the respectability of association with one of the most accomplished and celebrated of the early Persian poets, and he suggested a date for the ruba'i's 'discovery'. Rudaki died in A.D. 940.

The ruba'i's popularity can be accounted for by more than weariness of long courtly poems, with their carefully manipulated conventional sequences of regret over separation from a beloved person that merged into praises of a Sultan or notable. Persian poets handled this traditional ordering of the eulogy with a skill that enabled them to vary it ingeniously, but at the price of increasingly artificial diction. Ordinary people needed something more direct and simple. They found it in the ruba'i. Poets themselves needed a means of expression in which they would not have to suppress personal feelings, beliefs and doubts. Composed neither in hope of a potentate's reward nor in fear of his anger if the composition offended, ruba'is were circulated anonymously and often voiced criticism of fanatically imposed prohibitions and doctrine. The hypocrisy and lack of genuine human understanding frequently displayed by arid scholastics and wrangling religious jurisprudents were mocked. A ruba'i could easily be memorized, and as easily imitated. It could be recited in coteries of like-minded people, both for entertainment and to afford relief from oppression through private derision of pharasaically maintained dogmas.

Thus the ruba'i became a favourite verse form among intellec-
tuals, those philosophers and mystics in eleventh- and twelfth-
century Persia who were in some degree non-conformists opposed
to religious fanaticism, so that they have often been called Islam's
free-thinkers. Ruba'is which have survived consequently present a
wide variety of ideas, while precise identification of their authors is
often difficult. The ideas range from the religious to extremes of
scepticism. A form which stays in the memory like a proverb lends
itself to the expression of religious belief and unbelief with equal
ease. Ruba'is can be as contradictory as proverbs, and Fitzgerald
was right when he commented on how they alternate between the
'Grave' and the 'Gay'. The Persian verses' pithy comments range
through the spectrum of nearly all the most fundamental and uni-
versally shared parts of human experience, which goes a long way
to explain why so many men and women have loved and learnt by
heart Fitzgerald's translations.

As the following section will indicate, the originals were com-
posed in north-eastern Persia at times when there was occasion for
pessimism and little room for a sense of security. Such joy as might
be found had to be relished to the full while its moment lasted.

Omar Khayyam's Times

Until 1941 Omar Khayyam's date of birth was unverified. Then
Swami Govinda Tirtha published *The Nectar of Grace: Omar
Khayyam's Life and Works*.[3] In it he established that Khayyam was
born on 18 May 1048, a date ascertained on the basis of a horoscope
for him contained in one of the earliest biographical notices of him,
but long ignored by scholars. The Soviet Academy of Sciences
Institute of Theoretical Astronomy found the calculations correct.[4]
Modern investigators have also agreed that the formerly disputed

3. Allahabad, 1941
4. See John Andrew Boyle, 'Omar Khayyam: Astronomer, Mathematician and
Poet', Bulletin of the John Rylands Library, Manchester, Vol. 52, no. 1, Autumn 1969,
p.31, n. 3.

year of Khayyam's death was 1131. These dates, 1048–1131, tell us that Khayyam lived when the Saljuq Turkish Sultans were extending and consolidating their power over Persia and when the effects of this power were particularly felt in Nishapur, Khayyam's birthplace.

Nishapur was the capital of Khurasan, the north-eastern province of Persia, and, in Khayyam's time, of Eastern Islam. Thus Khurasan, which in the eleventh century extended as far as the river Oxus, was the first region to suffer when in 1031 Turkman tribes under their Saljuq chiefs entered Persia from beyond the river. In 1040 they occupied Nishapur and began to extend their dominion over Persia and Mesopotamia.

Khurasan was commercially rich. Its principal cities lay on trade routes which extended from the Far East through Persia to the Mediterranean. It was also fertile and so attracted invasion by the nomadic peoples of Central Asia once their tribal hosts had come as far west as the river Oxus. Throughout the Middle Ages the inhabitants of Khurasan were taught painful lessons in sudden reversals of fortune. Its people were threatened by the incursions of tribesmen who initially had little understanding of the life of settled cultivators or the communities of rich cities.

The name 'Khayyam' means 'tent-maker'. It belonged to Omar's father, Ibrahim, so that Omar seems to have sprung from the urban middle and manufacturing class of Nishapur society. Born only eight years after the Saljuq tribes' first crossing of the Oxus, he must have been brought up on stories of the sufferings of his city and the surrounding countryside. Between 1031 and 1040 the Saljuq Toghril Beg had finally occupied Nishapur and his Turkman troopers' horses had trampled irrigation works to pieces. Khurasan had been the scene of battles fought in a vain attempt to push the invaders back into Transoxiana. In 1040 Nishapur's notables had eagerly sought to come to terms with Toghril Beg, to insure as speedy a restoration of order as possible.[5]

5. See C. E. Bosworth, *The Ghaznavids: Their Empire in Afghanistan and Eastern Iran*, Edinburgh, 1963, Chaps. 5 and 6.

An intelligent man brought up on the memories of this invasion and destined to experience the full force of the new and alien régime's administration might well have been a pessimist. Any forebodings Khurasan's frontier position inspired in Khayyam's epoch were to be justified ninety years after his death when the province was again devastated, this time by the Mongols coming from the east under Chinghiz Khan. Saljuq power waned after 1157 and the province had already been ravaged by other Turkman tribes from the region of Khorezmia to the north before the Mongols' arrival. When, therefore, another Khurasanian poet, Minuchihri, who died about 1040, speaks of autumn and 'the cold breeze blowing from the Khorezmian quarter', it is easy to think he meant more than the wind. Like Khayyam he belonged to a society of cultured Persians living precariously under the menace of destructive marauders from the north and north-east.

Toghril Beg's main task after establishing himself in Nishapur was to define his position as Sultan of the lands of Eastern Islam in relation to this area's religious and legal sovereign, the Caliph of Baghdad. The Saljuqs professed Islam, the religion preached by the Prophet Muhammad in Arabia in the seventh century and brought to Persia in 642, a decade after the Prophet's death, by his Arab compatriots. The legal headship of the Faith had been vested since 750 in the Caliphs of Baghdad, who represented orthodox Islam. The Saljuq leader required that his secular power should be recognized by the Caliph in order that its legality might be sealed. Islam was both the Law and the Faith, and the Caliphs represented the continuation of what was termed the *Sunna*, the orthodox tradition of the doctrine and legal decisions which the Prophet had bequeathed to the Muslim community.

By 1062 Toghril Beg's negotiations with Baghdad had succeeded and he could declare himself 'The Reviver of Islam', 'The Caliph's Right Hand', and 'King of the East and West'. This meant that Omar Khayyam and his contemporaries found themselves living under a renewed if not unprecedentedly forceful application of the principles of Islamic law. When it is remembered that this law includes the prohibition of wine and drunkenness, it will be seen that many of the ruba'is translated below were heretical. The law was enforced by religious officials responsible to the Caliphate and supported by the Saljuq Sultans. These officials were Islam's nearest equivalent to a priesthood, which Islam lacked, Islamic orthodoxy admitting no human intermediary between God and Man. These 'Shaikhs', as the doctors of Muslim law were called, shared the scorn poured by the ruba'is on the prohibition of wine, and on decrees of the Faith in general.

Sufis and Philosophers

Islam was, however, disturbed by many factions. Its territories also contained members of the three other religions it tolerated, Judaism, Christianity, and the old religion of Persia, Zoroastrianism. Jews, Christians and Zoroastrians were present in Nishapur, which in the eleventh century was riven by factionalism among the Muslims themselves. References in the ruba'is to the 'Two and Seventy Sects' reflect contemporary phenomena, the religious and legal wrangling of Muslims of different schools. In addition, there were traces of cults left over from pre-Islamic Persia but differing from Zoroastrianism. In the eighth and early ninth centuries Khurasan had been the scene of a spate of rebellions in a religious guise against Islamic orthodoxy and Arab rule. Khayyam would be acquainted with the pretensions of the kind of illuminati who had led these movements, but by his time their ideas had largely been absorbed into Sufism, one of whose greatest exponents, the Khurasanian Abu Sa'id ibn Abi'l-Khair, had been influential in Nishapur. He died in 1049.

The word *Sufi* originates in the Arabic for 'wool', *suf*. Adherents of Sufism wore a distinctive woollen cloak. Since they professed poverty, they were also called *Dervishes*; *dervish* means 'poor'. More moderate Sufis strove to present themselves as good Sunnis, upholders of the *Sunna*, orthodox Islam, but Sufis varied from strict pietists and moderates to extremists best described as 'Lords of Misrule'. This variety makes it hard to define Sufism with any degree of precision, but if the eremitic extreme at one end of the scale and the sybaritic at the other are excluded, a central or 'moderate' position becomes discernible.

Sufism's motive force is love. This love cannot be quite equated with agape. Nor is it simply eros. The dichotomy between these two does not seem to have been present to the Persian mind. What the Persians call *'Ishq*, the passion of love, was directed in Sufism solely towards God the Creator. This channelling of love exclusively towards the Creator derived its sanction from a saying attributed to the Prophet Muhammad in explanation of God's act of creation. God said, 'I was a Hidden Treasure and I desired to be known, so that I made the Creature that I might be known.'[6]

Implicit in this saying is the notion that the whole of God's creation is an epiphany, and Sufi poetry does not lack what in the West would be called pantheism. Whether the ruba'is translated below are in some instances to be taken as contrary to the Sufi position or not, the frequent imagery of mortal clay turned into pots, or of flowers and the edges of brooks which were once human lips and limbs, can be considered pantheistic. But the emphasis is on Man rather than on God, and in Persian thought it is not so much a matter of 'pantheism' as of the sense that all the elements of God's creation – of nature – are inextricably and sympathetically combined. Thus the 'pantheism' in the imagery of Persian poetry cannot be taken unreservedly as representing what is meant by this term in the West. Its origins lie in a deeply rooted Oriental acceptance of nature's oneness, a concept which may or may not include belief in a divine Creator in or outside the natural order.

From ancient times Persia was a crossroads between East and West, so that as well as teachers acquainted with Greek ideas it produced others influenced by the Orient. This gives a clue to Sufism's eclecticism. Khurasan was especially exposed to ideas from Central Asia and India, and in the tenth century, following a proscription against freedom of philosophical inquiry in Baghdad, its cities began to assume Baghdad's former role as a centre of philosophical speculation. Cities such as Marv and Bokhara, which

6. E. J. W. Gibb, *History of Ottoman Poetry*, Vol. 1, London, 1900 and 1958, p.17.

were in the old greater Khurasan, had begun since the middle of the ninth century to enjoy a measure of political freedom from the Caliphs of Baghdad, though still subject to them as the legal heads of Islam. This freedom made it possible for scholars who fled from persecution in the Caliph's capital to find refuge in Khurasan, where schools and libraries flourished in a manner indicative of the major part played in the intellectual life of Islam by astute and inquiring Persians.

Had the people of north-eastern Persia not needed a palliative against the sufferings occasioned by invasion and against the rigours of the Islamic legalism the Saljuq government tried to impose, Sufism might have remained a branch of the religious and philosophical inquiries of a few adepts. In the event Khurasan became the cradle of the highest forms of philosophical Sufism, which developed alongside the more extreme forms characteristic of popular and ecstatic sects. It also became the seat of rationalist thinkers influenced by Aristotle and the neo-Platonic commentators. Later the breakdown of law and order gave further impetus to popular forms of Sufism and eventually resulted in philosophy's debasement.

The basic Sufi teaching of love directed exclusively towards God required the utmost piety and asceticism. The physical world's attractions diverted the soul of man from concentration on the Creator. They were a veil between God and Man. The latter's lament was over his sense of separation from the Beloved. His purpose was to avoid the beguilements of the phenomenal and unabiding world, so that the soul might be free to attain knowledge of the only certitude and truth: God was the sole reality. Asceticism was a primary feature of Sufi discipline, because the world's distractions multiplied with the indulgence of appetites.

Many in the East, however, did not draw the sharp distinction known in the West between the physical and the psychical, and the exaltation of spiritual love in Sufism became in Sufism's more popular forms a licence for a libertinism believed to be authorized by love's superiority over all law. Moreover, with its increasing appeal to the masses in eleventh-century Khurasan, Sufism became a social force, as well as the spiritual exercise it had been when restricted to a few rigorously trained initiates. Sufi leaders gathered fraternities round themselves, organized into a network of hospice-like centres called *Khangahs*. The khangah was a refuge, not only for the seeker of spiritual peace through renunciation of the world, but also for those who sought the communal reassurance membership of a brotherhood can confer.

Gradually the khangahs became focal points in the rehabilitation of a population which invasions such as the Mongols' decimated and terrified. In some Sufi Orders the novice was taught the first essentials of social survival, learning how to tailor clothes, make boots and candles, mill corn and bake bread. The Mongol invaders, when they did not massacre them, carried off craftsmen as captives. When sources of production had been destroyed and had to be revitalized, the Sufis set about making it possible for life to be resumed.

When Persia's invaders ceased destroying and settled in a conquered area, they began to exploit it ruthlessly. An already reduced and impoverished population was burdened with taxes it had little means of paying. As part of asceticism, poverty was one of the professions of Sufism, but where many people were so bitterly poor, poverty did not have to be professed – it was unavoidable. The notables of Nishapur charged the Sufi Abu Sa'id with extravagance, held up in the *Koran* as a sin hateful to God. This charge came from Abu Sa'id's practice of entertaining his followers to sumptuous banquets. He himself was reputed to live like a prince. Such a style of life does not seem to match Sufi professions of poverty and avoidance of the world's delights, but if we remember that the physical and psychical worlds were not sharply differentiated, and that Sufism was providing the oppressed and hungry with hope and sustenance, the paradox is lost. In any event, so far as the Sufi Elect were concerned, once the perfect knowledge of God had been attained – this was not vouchsafed to all, but only to the most courageous and persevering – then the world God created was both to be enjoyed and to be made tolerable for the Sufi's fellow creatures.

It was not long before Sufism was affected by the desire for conformity common in the period of the Saljuq Sultans. Systematizers sought to bring Sufism into line with the Faith. Al-Ghazali, the philosopher whose meeting with Khayyam will shortly be described and who was opposed to the 'Greek Learning', was a pioneer in the endeavour to assimilate Sufism into orthodox Islam. He was followed by lesser men, one of whom, Najmu'd-Din Daya, as we shall see when we discuss the ruba'is, virulently attacked Khayyam. He charged him with gross aberration from the requirements of religion and dubbed him a materialist incapable of following the Sufi path to knowledge of the divine. In the eyes of both Al-Ghazali and this relatively undistinguished schoolman of a century later, Khayyam's chief fault was that he was one of the philosophers who followed the eleventh-century Persian polymath Ibn Sina, famous in Christendom as Avicenna, and through him the learning of the Greeks, by which was meant Aristotle and the Neo-Platonists.

We shall also have occasion to notice an attack on Khayyam in one of the poems of a man very different from the scholastics, an inspired Sufi poet and far from orthodox. He was Faridu'd-Din 'Attar, Khayyam's fellow-townsman, born only a decade after his death. He narrates a supposed vision of Khayyam in the afterlife, ashamed and confused on being rejected at God's threshold. There his 'knowledge' availed him nothing, having only made him deficient in those spiritual qualities without which no one can be blessed by God's acceptance. Thus Khayyam stood condemned alike by the spiritually and intellectually tolerant Sufi poet, from whom, exceptionally, he received no compassion because he was so heinously a materialist, and by the Sufi schoolman, who abhorred him as a spurner of religion, lacking the grace to attain the Sufi's gnostic beatitude.

Persian materialism has attracted less attention in the West than Persian religion, but realism and empiricism are just as characteristic of the Persians as is spirituality. In modern times westerners have sometimes felt the need to find an escape from the western dualism of spiritual as contrasted with materialist concepts. Seeking an alternative to occidental materialism, they have turned to oriental literature, the recourse of Europeans for whom the Christian religious heritage no longer suffices. Going to the Persian Parnassus for spiritual truths, they have closed their eyes to the fact that in Persia what is spiritual and abstract is inextricably woven into a thoroughly pragmatic assessment of life's values and chances. Under the bright skies and glittering stars of Persia, heaven and earth seem so close that it is hard to distinguish between what is heavenly and what earthly. One may be the only reality, but the other can ideally be that reality's mirror.

Fitzgerald was an exception among nineteenth-century explorers of Persian poetry, because he was not looking for a spiritual solace which, in any event, his profound scepticism would have precluded. He was clear in his grasp of the often very austere and unconsoling message of many of the ruba'is he chose to translate. Whether or not Omar Khayyam was the author of all the ruba'is Fitzgerald took up can be left aside – what matters is Fitzgerald's deep understanding of the mind of a medieval Khurasanian mathematician and philosopher such as we must now show Khayyam to have been.

Omar Khayyam, Philosopher and Mathematician

The earliest references to Khayyam do not give any indication that he was a poet, but establish him as a philosopher, and works by him still extant prove him to have been a great mathematician.

In a treatise composed in the second decade of the twelfth century the philologist Az-Zamakhshari mentioned that Omar Khayyam visited one of his classes and was acquainted with the Arabic stanzas of the Syrian poet Al-Ma'arri, who died when Khayyam was about ten years old. Al-Ma'arri's contempt for hypocrisy resembled 'Omar Khayyam's, and the imagery and sentiments of his epigrammatical verses are strikingly like the ruba'is which have come down to us under Khayyam's name.[7]

7. For the discovery of this reference and the proposal that it was by Az-Zamakhshari (d.1141), see Badi'uz-Zaman Firuzanfar, Bulletin of the Faculty of

Az-Zamakhshari's remarks about Omar Khayyam ante-date the other two descriptions of him which have survived, written by contemporaries who knew him. The first of these is contained in a book called the *Chahar Maqaleh* ('Four Discourses'), written about 1155–6 by Nizami 'the Prosodist' of Samarqand.[8] This work comprises discourses on secretaryship, poets, astrologers and physicians. It is a compendium written as a guide for the accomplished young man desirous of making his way as a chancellory and court servant to a medieval Muslim Prince. While the chapter on poets includes beautiful examples of fine panegyric poetry, and short stanzas aimed to prove poetry's power over the minds of peevish or disgruntled rulers, it does not discuss the ruba'i, nor does it allude to Khayyam. The reference to him occurs in the section on astrologers.

It is not to be wondered at that contemporary biographers of Khayyam are silent about the ruba'is. In the twelfth century no Persian's fame rested on the composition of ruba'is alone. Whether or not they also composed ruba'is, great poets were celebrated for their more ample productions. Philosophers like Khayyam and Avicenna, whom he followed, had ruba'is attributed to them, but their fame rested not on these but on their philosophical writings. In any event, it would not strike Nizami the Prosodist as appropriate to mention ruba'is of a distinctly unorthodox and uncourtly type in an essay devoted to teaching civil servants and courtiers how deftly turned verses might beneficially influence the hearts of princes.

Khayyam was famous as an astronomer, so that in the age in which he lived he was bound to be commanded to make astrologi-

---

Letters, Tabriz, Vol. 1, 1948–9, pp.1–29. E. G. Browne (*Literary History of Persia*, Vol. II, London, 1906, and Cambridge, 1956, p.292) saw the resemblance between Al-Ma'arri's verses and the ruba'is long before Professor Firuzanfar discovered Az-Zamakhshari's reference to Khayyam and his acquaintance with the Arab sceptic.

8. *Chahar Maqaleh*, ed. Qazvini, revised with additional notes by Muhammad Mu'in, Teheran, 1954–5; E. G. Browne, *Revised Translation of the Chahar Maqala* [*sic*], Cambridge and Leyden, 1921.

cal predictions. Nizami states that Omar did not have 'any great belief in astrological predictions; nor have I seen or heard of any great men who has such belief'. In being sceptical of astrology, Khayyam was in tune with Avicenna, who wrote a book refuting it. Nizami cites one occasion when Khayyam was ordered to make a prediction and did so in circumstances that enabled him to rely on meteorology rather than astrology. In the year 1114 a Saljuq prince asked Khayyam to select a time when the days would be fine for a royal hunting expedition. Khayyam chose days which, after a storm on the first morning, remained free of rain and snow, proving his forecast correct.

Another 'prediction' made by Khayyam is the substance of Nizami's moving account of a meeting with him in the city of Balkh in the year 1112 or 1113. Nizami says he had been Khayyam's pupil and that the last time he saw him was by chance at a friend's house in the Street of the Slave-sellers in Balkh. There, in the midst of a 'convivial gathering', Khayyam prophesied that his grave would be in a spot 'where the trees will shed their blossoms on me twice a year'. This seemed impossible to Nizami, 'though I knew that one such as he would not speak idle words'. Nizami went to Nishapur some twenty-three years later, four years after Omar Khayyam had died in 1131. He found his grave situated beneath a garden wall over which pear and peach trees were leaning. So much blossom had fallen that the grave was completely hidden by it. Nizami, recalling what Khayyam had said in Balkh, wept for his old master.

Sometime between 1158 and 1170, within forty years of Khayyam's death, 'Ali ibn Zaidu'l-Baihaqi compiled a collection of the lives and works of eminent philosophers and included a biography of Khayyam, besides scattered references throughout the work which illustrate Khayyam's philosophy.[9]

'Ali ibn Zaid heads the biography, 'The Teacher, Philosopher and Authority on the Truth 'Umar ibn Ibrahim al-Khayyam' (Omar

9. Zahir'd-Din Abu'l-Hasan Ali ibn Zaidu'l-Baihaqi, *Tatimma Siwanu'l-Hikma* ('Supplement to the Bibliotheca Philosophica'), Arabic text ed. Muhammad Shafi', Lahore, 1935. Cf. Muhammad Shafi', 'The Author of the Oldest Biographical Notice of 'Umar Khayyam', in *Islamic Culture*, Vol. VI, 1932, pp.586–623.

son of Ibrahim the tent-maker). This heading is no help to the student who wants evidence that Khayyam composed ruba'is, nor is anything else that 'Ali ibn Zaid has to say about him. He establishes Khayyam as one of the great rationalist philosophers of his time, without reference to poetry.

The words 'Authority on the Truth' translate the form of title, *Hujjatu'l-Haqq*, applied only to foremost men of learning. It was the title given to Avicenna, to whom alone, according to 'Ali ibn Zaid, Khayyam was second as the perfect master of all the exact and philosophical sciences of his day. 'Ali ibn Zaid says he was a child of eight when his father introduced him to Khayyam, who tested the boy by making him construe a verse of Arabic poetry and define the different varieties of curved lines. His account is not altogether friendly. Khayyam is described as 'narrow-minded and cantankerous', and his reluctance to produce books or receive pupils is emphasized. It is possible that 'Ali ibn Zaid, who outlived him by many years, was taking care not to appear too zealous a partisan of Khayyam in the eyes of his enemies.

'Ali ibn Zaid narrates a meeting between Khayyam and the philosopher Al-Ghazali which seems to have been unfruitful and unfriendly. Al-Ghazali wrote a work, *Tahafutu'l-Falasifa* ('Destructio philosophorum'), which aimed to demolish the philosophy of Avicenna. It would have been surprising if this opponent of the 'Greek Learning' had felt any sympathy for a man like Khayyam, whom he somewhat perfunctorily asked a question on astronomy. Khayyam's answer was so prolix that he appeared to be dodging the issue, and he had not finished speaking when a muezzin gave the call to midday prayers from a nearby mosque. Al-Ghazali immediately rose to his feet and said, 'Truth has come and falsehood vanished; verily what is false is bound to vanish,' a quotation from the *Koran*[10] by which Al-Ghazali implied the falsity of Khayyam's opinions.

Al-Ghazali refuted Avicenna on no less than twenty points, and it is interesting to note that at least three of these – and very

---

10. *Koran*, Chap. XVII, verse 83.

important ones – are alluded to in the ruba'is attributed to Khayyam. The first is unbelief in orthodox Islamic eschatology, especially in the resurrection of the body after death, a cardinal Muslim tenet. The possibility of an afterlife is constantly questioned in the ruba'is. The second is the belief of philosophers of Avicenna's school that God could know only essences or universals, not the particulars of things. The philosophers followed Aristotle and Plotinus in believing that God was a simple, incorporeal unity with which diversification of knowledge of specific entities would be incompatible, but in which the essences of all things were implicit. This belief was utterly repugnant to orthodox Muslims because it conflicted with the teaching that God created all things in their individual forms, and because it was alleged to suggest a limitation in the Omniscient's knowledge.

A fundamentalist allegation of this kind provides a clue to what Khayyam meant when, 'Ali ibn Zaid tells us, he accused one of Avicenna's critics of failing to understand that teacher's terms. Khayyam was engaged in a dispute with a philosophical opponent in the presence of the ruler of Yazd, a city in southern Persia. He offended the ruler by his defence of Avicenna and contempt for this opponent, a man the prince favoured. Arguments about whether God knew only universals, or particulars as well, are alluded to in several of the ruba'is in this book, notably number 188; but the poet suggests that drinking wine is better than worrying about such matters.

The third point which particularly aroused orthodox ire was Avicenna's theory that the earth is uncreated, based on the belief that it is coeval or 'continuous' with the Unmovable Mover, Himself incorporeal and outside time, so that the world too must be eternal and uncreated. The orthodox accused philosophers of Avicenna's and the Greek School of denying the fact of creation, by which God made Himself known to man. This denial of earth's creation and the belief that God could only know universals led to the charge that the philosophers were really atheists. In Ruba'i 93 below, the contention about whether or not the world is created in time or eternal is dismissed because when we are dead it will be the same, created or uncreated.

Leaving aside his description of Khayyam's personal traits, the picture 'Ali ibn Zaid gives of him is that of a typical medieval polymath, versed in all sciences, including medicine, but chiefly notable as an exponent of the 'Greek Learning'. The two ruba'is just referred to in fact suggest impatience at wrangling over speculative philosophy; such problems are dismissed and hedonism preferred. But it has to be remembered that Khayyam was primarily a practical philosopher and mathematician. His treatise on the difficulties of Euclid's Elements advanced the theory of numbers and is still extant.[11] As a young man barely in his mid twenties, he wrote his famous treatise on algebra, demonstrating for the first time how to solve cubic equations.[12]

In the introduction to this work Khayyam says that the rigours the genuinely learned suffered in his time were so severe that they could only afford to specialize in research in one branch of science, which to a medieval polymath would be an irksome restriction. He continues, 'Most of our so-called scholars forfeit truth for falsehood, never passing beyond the bounds of imposture and speciousness. The little learning they have, they exploit for the meanest gain. If they see a man searching for the truth, diligent in honesty and the eradication of folly and exposure of guile, they deride and belittle him.' A comment of this kind seems to explain why, as a much older man than when he wrote these words, Khayyam appeared cantankerous and 'niggardly' in writing books and teaching.

In 1074 Khayyam was among the astronomers summoned by the Saljuq Sultan Jalalu'd-Din Malikshah and his famous minister Nizamu'l-Mulk to revise the calendar and construct an observatory. A new era was fixed, known as the Jalali or Maliki Era. New Year's Day was shifted from the point of the sun's passage through the

11. See *Cambridge History of Iran*, Vol. V, 1968, p.663.
12. See F. Woepke, *L'Algèbre de Omar Alkhayyami*, Paris, 1851 (Arabic text and French translation); D. S. Kasir, *The Algebra of Omar Khayyam*, New York, 1951; and *Cambridge History of Iran*, Vol. V, pp.665–6.

middle point of Pisces to the first point of Aries, and the New Era was inaugurated on 16 March A.D. 1079. Gibbon described it as comparable for accuracy with the Gregorian style of dating.[13]

With reference to the great vizier Nizamu'l-Mulk, there is an old legend according to which he, Khayyam and the heresiarch religio-political leader Hasan Sabbah, who founded an 'Order of Assassins' to plague the Saljuq government, were schoolfriends, but Nizamu'l-Mulk would have been thirty when Khayyam was born, and Khayyam and Sabbah's paths do not seem ever to have crossed. In condemnations of Khayyam as a philosopher of the Greek School there is no hint of his being tainted with the Isma'ili heresy of which Hasan Sabbah was the chief missionary in Persia, where the movement spread terror from 1090 until 1256, when Hulagu Khan the Mongol suppressed it. (See Appendix 1.)

In devising the new calendar Khayyam enjoyed the patronage of the Saljuq Sultan, but 'Ali ibn Zaid provides evidence of hostility to him from a successor of Malikshah, the Sultan Sanjar. Sanjar was governor of Khurasan from 1117, and Sultan from 1137 until his death in 1157. Though he died before Sanjar became Sultan, Khayyam would have been subject to him as governor of Khurasan for a number of years. These may well have been difficult years, since 'Ali ibn Zaid tells us Sanjar had in his infancy conceived a 'hatred' for Khayyam. As a child Sanjar was ill. Khayyam, asked to make a prognosis, said the ailment was fatal. A slave reported Khayyam's gloomy verdict to the Prince, who never forgave it.

'Ali ibn Zaid is the source for Khayyam's horoscope, from which, as has been noted, a modern Indian scholar established his date of birth. He is also the source for the description of Khayyam's last moments which later historians have copied. The philosopher was reading from Avicenna's *Book of Healing* the chapter on metaphysics where it deals with 'the One and the Many'. He marked the place with a gold toothpick and called his household together to hear his Will and last instructions. He then said prayers,

---

13. *Decline and Fall of the Roman Empire*, Bury's edition, Vol. VI, Chap. LVII, p.246.

and before expiring made his peace with God, saying, 'Oh Lord, I have known You according to the sum of my ability. Pardon me since verily my knowledge is my recommendation to You.' Critics say that a story of this kind might have been designed to enhance Khayyam's posthumous reputation, exculpating him from charges of heresy and atheism, but it was as a philosopher that Khayyam was presenting himself to God, knowledge his only claim to grace. The contention of his Sufi castigator Faridu'd-Din 'Attar was that this knowledge was not what God required.

Khayyam and the Ruba'is

The first work to mention Khayyam as a poet is an Arabic compilation about poets and their art called the *Kharidatu'l-Qasr* ('Virgin Pearl of the Palace'), written in 1176–7 by Katibu'l-Isfahani ('the Clerk of Isfahan'). Khayyam is cited as one of the poets of Khurasan, a man 'peerless in his time and without equal in astronomy and philosophy, so that he is proverbial'. There is, however, no reference to his having composed Persian ruba'is; the only example given of his poetical composition consists of four verses in Arabic.

This reference to Khayyam in the context of poetry is slight, but important because written only forty-five years after his death, which lends it authenticity. In the *History of Philosophers*, the abridgment made in 1249 by Az-Zauzani of al-Qifti's *News of the Learned with Reports of the Sages*, Khayyam is described as a composer of 'fugitive verses' which were 'a tissue of error like poisonous snakes' in the eyes of the Canon Law. The author says that these verses' inner meaning revealed the evil of Khayyam's mind and that he was threatened with execution on the charge of heresy, so that he went on the Pilgrimage to Mecca, prudently drawing in 'the reins of his tongue and pen'. The citation describes Khayyam as a follower of Greek science and exponent of Greek culture.[14]

14. Al-Qifti, abridged by Az-Zauzani *Tarikhu'l Hukama'*, ed. J. Lippert, Leipzig, 1903, pp.243–4.

Al-Qifti was born in Egypt and died in Syria in 1248, which means that he lived and worked in regions west of Persia and Mesopotamia and not threatened by the Mongols, who first devastated northern Persia in 1220, until some twelve years after al-Qifti had died. It was to Syria that some of the scholars fleeing from Khurasan in 1220 after Chinghiz Khan's arrival there went to find asylum. One was the eminent geographer Yaqut. In 1221 he escaped from the Mongols' sack of the Khurasanian city of Marv and wrote a description of the terrors of the invasion in a letter to al-Qifti. He particularly lamented the destruction of Marv's superb libraries and it is possible that a work like al-Qifti's anthology of philosophers may have been inspired by Yaqut's doleful report of what had happened in north-eastern Persia. It must have seemed a matter of urgency, since so many of their remains had been destroyed, that the names, accomplishments and works of philosophers who had adorned Islamic society before the Mongols' coming should be recorded for posterity.

Similarly, thirteenth-century historians felt impelled to record the disaster the Mongols brought to Islamic civilization. In 1260 Juvaini completed his *History of the World Conqueror*, a narrative of the Mongols from Chinghiz Khan to the time of his grandson Hulagu's conquest of north Persia and Mesopotamia in 1256–8.[15] Juvaini mentions how, after the sack of Marv, a group of survivors counted the dead. In thirteen days they had counted over a million corpses and it was then, the historians tells us, that they recited a ruba'i, 'of Omar Khayyam', number 44 below, as 'suitable to the occasion'.[16] Juvaini thus provides one of the earliest examples of a ruba'i attributed to Khayyam.

Four or five ruba'is which posterity has attributed to Khayyam appeared before Juvaini's time in the *Sindbad Nameh*, a book of fables believed to be of Indian origin and produced in Persian prose

15. Juvaini, *History of the World Conqueror*, translated by J. A. Boyle, Manchester, 1958.

16. Juvaini, *Tarikh-i-Jahan Gushay*, Vol. 1, Leyden and London, 1912, p.128; and Boyle's translation, *op. cit.*, Vol. 1, p.164. Juvaini's text of the original ruba'i varies slightly from the original of no. 44.

in 1160–61, and the *Marzuban Nameh*, written about 1225.[17] Both these works are collections of tales for entertainment and to point a moral. The ruba'is are cited in them as rhymes expressive of common human joys and sorrows, and too commonplace to warrant ascribing them to any particular author. Khayyam's name is not mentioned in either work.

Two ruba'is are explicitly stated to be his in the polemical work composed in 1223 by Najmu'd-Din Daya, the Sufi scholastic already mentioned. His book was intended to uphold Sufism as an orthodox development of Islamic doctrine and to condemn the errors of false Sufis and the faithless. It is called *Mirsadu'l 'Ibad* ('Watch Tower of Devotees'), and in it two ruba'is are fathered on Khayyam because cited specifically to exemplify his wickedness.[18] They are numbers 10 and 11 in the collection translated below, and run as follows:

> The cycle which includes our coming and going
> Has no discernible beginning nor end;
> Nobody has got this matter straight –
> Where we come from and where we go to.

> Since the Upholder embellishes the material of things,
> For what reason does He cast it into diminution and decay?
> If it turned out good, why break it?
> If the form turned out bad, whose fault was it?

The polemical purpose of this work unfortunately raises doubts about the attribution of these two ruba'is to Omar Khayyam. It would be easy for an enemy merely to quote verses that were to hand as evidence of unbelief; but at the same time the very appositeness of the two ruba'is chosen must be taken as proof that,

17. *Sindbad Nameh*, ed. Ahmad Ateş, Istanbul, 1948; *Marzuban Nameh*, ed. Qazvini, Tehran, 1938–9. The latter was translated as *The Tales of Marzuban* by Reuben Levy, London, 1959.

18. *Mirsadu'l 'Ibad*, ed. Husaini Shamsu'l 'Urafa', Tehran, 1933, pp.18 and 27. Cf. E. G. Browne, *Revised Translation of the Chahar Maqala*, Cambridge and London, 1921, pp.135–6.

in some circles at least, Khayyam was notorious as a heretic and also reputed to be a composer of ruba'is.

By the fourteenth century efforts to salvage the literary remains of the civilization the Mongols had destroyed gave rise to the production of anthologies. In one of these, the *Nuzhatu'l-Majalis* ('Delight of Assemblies'), dated 1330–31, twenty-one ruba'is are given as by Khayyam. In another, the *Mu'nisu'l-Ahrar fi Daqa'iqu'l Ash'ar* ('The Noble Men's Companion to Verses' Subtleties') of 1340–41, thirteen ruba'is are attributed to him. Those thus attributed in both these compilations are all included in the translations below.[19] Other fourteenth-century manuscript collections of ruba'is also contain items ascribed to Khayyam, but the two mentioned here are the best known, with the Bodleian Manuscript used by Fitzgerald and copied in Shiraz in 1460–61.

Several of the ruba'is attributed to Khayyam in these manuscripts also appear in ancient books as the compositions of other famous twelfth-century Persian poets and philosophers, and in some instances they have been attributed to later poets too. Thus it is impossible to rely absolutely on the attributions of post-Mongol Persian anthologists. Where the same poem is attributed to more than one well-known writer it is difficult to avoid the suspicion that the early anthologists were often as uncertain about the ruba'is' authorship as modern scholars are. The fame of an Avicenna or Omar Khayyam would make it easy for philosophical verses to be put under their names. The notoriety of their unorthodox views would result in unorthodox ruba'is being attributed to them, though such attributions would in all probability not have been made in the absence of rumour that such men did from time to time strike off verses of this type.

At the end of the day we seem to be left with the ruba'i Juvaini attributed to Khayyam as the only one to be accepted as his. The

19. Cf. Jalalud-Din Huma'i (ed.), *Tarabkhaneh* ('House of Merriment'), Tehran, 1342/1963. This is a fifteenth-century selection of Khayyam's ruba'is made by Rashid of Tabriz. Huma'i discusses earlier collections in considerable detail in his Introduction.

historian had no reason to fabricate Khayyam's authorship of the God-chiding stanza the survivors at Marv recited as 'suitable to the occasion'. The Sufi scholastic Najmu'd-Din Daya, on the other hand, quoted the other two ruba'is most early attributed to him with the motive of destroying Khayyam's reputation.

In his article, 'The Earliest Collections of O. Khayyam',[20] the late Professor Minorsky accepted Najmu'd-Din's two attributions along with Juvaini's when he said that before 1949 scholars had been able to recognize three ruba'is only as definitely by Khayyam. He was discussing the three collections of ruba'is purporting to be Khayyam's which appeared in Europe and America between 1949 and 1952 in manuscripts dated 1208, 1216 and 1259. These manuscripts were hailed by scholars as the means of ascertaining at last which ruba'is were incontrovertibly Khayyam's. The manuscript dated 1259 was edited and published in 1949.[21] That which was supposed to have been written 'only seventy-five years after Omar's death', in 1208-9, was translated and published in 1952.[22] But when the third manuscript, said to date from the year 1216, appeared very soon after the others, and when the other two had been more closely scrutinized, the genuineness of all three compilations began to be doubted. They are now no longer accepted as authentic.

The problems of the authorship of the ruba'is known as Khayyam's have exercised scholars ever since Fitzgerald's translations achieved fame, but it is not our purpose to pursue these problems here. Nor is it our purpose to continue discussion, more recently engaging students of Khayyam, about whether or not he was a Sufi. What one Sufi writer had to say about him and two of his ruba'is in 1223 has just been mentioned, and, as we have already seen, the great Sufi poet 'Attar described how on reaching God's threshold Khayyam's learning was no substitute for the spiritual

20. In *Yádnáme-ye Jan Rypka*, Prague, 1967, pp.107–18.
21. A. J. Arberry (ed.), *The Ruba'iyat of Omar Khayyam*, Emery Walker, 1949.
22. A. J. Arberry, *Omar Khayyam*, London 1952.

grace and faith he lacked.[23] If Khayyam was a Sufi, he was certainly not the sort either 'Attar or Najmu'd-Din Daya would extol; but Sufi eclecticism makes it dangerous to be dogmatic about matters of this kind. (See Appendix 2.)

These problems apart,[24] the two selections from which the following translations have been made share the merit of having been compiled by three men who, though they lived centuries after Khayyam, were fellow-Persians speaking his language as their mother tongue. Sadiq Hedayat published his selection of the ruba'is in 1934. That of Muhammad 'Ali Furughi and Qasim Ghani, which includes many ruba'is also chosen by Hedayat, was published in 1942. Of these two selections Hedayat's is the more convincing to anybody concerned with literature rather than with whether or not Khayyam composed all or some of the poems. Hedayat was himself a creative writer and his sound literary sense made him generally choose ruba'is of firm poetic quality, only occasionally marred by inconsistencies in ideas or style. The chief virtue of his selection – the first 143 of the translations below – is that it best exemplifies the directness of diction and enamel-bright vision of nature characteristic of pre-Mongol Persian poetry.

This directness preceded the excessive use of abstract conceits and play upon words. It avoided far-fetched allusions combined with lack of concision and force. The presence or absence of this

23. H. Ritter (ed.), *Ilahi-Nameh* ('Book of the Divinity'), Istanbul, 1940, p.272, lines 12–15. Cf. John Andrew Boyle, 'Omar Khayyam: Astronomer, Mathematician and Poet', in Bulletin of the John Rylands Library, Manchester, Vol. 52, no. 1, Autumn 1969, p.45.

24. Huma'i (see p.28, no. 19) discusses the problems of ruba' is' authorship with great skill and authority, while J. A. Boyle in the article 'Omar Khayyam: Astronomer, Mathematician and Poet' cited in note 23 above discusses the question of Khayyam's relationship to Sufism. It should, however, be said that al-Qifti, in the compendium of lives of philosophers referred to earlier, does state that Khayyam believed in the necessity for 'the purification of the bodily functions, to release the human soul from carnal associations in the quest for the Unique Judge', that is, the One. This sounds like Neo-Platonism: it postulates a Pythagorean–Neo-Platonic background to certain manifestations of Sufism with which Khayyam, according to the passage in question from al-Qifti, could be associated.

directness and natural realism are the criteria by which to judge whether a ruba'i was composed before the thirteenth century and the Mongol catastrophe and is therefore attributable to Khayyam. At the same time it must not be forgotten that many ruba'is we know as coming from the eleventh and twelfth centuries were in all probability inherited from earlier periods, part of a legacy to which Khayyam and his contemporaries were heirs. We should be thankful today that any of these poems have survived at all to bring into our own age a Persian clarity, courage and beauty.

Peter Avery
Cambridge

The following translations are intended to give as literal an English version of the Persian originals as readability and intelligibility permit. It seemed important to try and convey the baldness of the originals. Past translations of Persian verse have often tended to blur and soften the hard directness of the Persian, allowing a sentimentality quite absent from the original to intrude. It is hoped that these translations will answer the question a Persianist is often asked: 'What do the Persian originals of the ruba'is really say?' On the other hand, there is no need to disparage the famous version of Edward Fitzgerald. His work is more in the nature of a fantasia than a translation. It is often very free and occasionally not precisely accurate. But Fitzgerald's poetic intuition guided him aright in divining the essentially sceptical and unorthodox nature of the Persian poet's thought. He gave to the ruba'is a Victorian richness and lushness of sentiment which was alien to them, but he was also a champion of such Augustan poets as Dryden and Crabbe at a period when their merits were often under-valued. His study of them gave to his work on Persian originals a concision and wit which were entirely appropriate, and which his imitators have completely failed to emulate.

In the translations offered here the intervention of the diction and convention of English verse has been eschewed, because such an intervention is felt to widen the distance between the English reader and the content and spirit of the original Persian text by interposing an extraneous poetical mode. Experience shows that where the original is of a high order and faithfully translated into plain English, the quality of the Persian poem raises the English prose above the level of the merely prosaic. Conversely, when the original is not of the best, and the selections used offer a variety of standards, faithful rendering into English reveals the weakness of the Persian poem. Differences in quality would be less apparent in translations put into the mould of English verse.

Sadiq Hedayat divided his selection into groups according to themes: 'The Mystery of Creation' (1–15), 'Life's Agony' (16–25), 'Destiny's Decree' (26–34), 'The Revolutions of Time' (35–56),

'Revolving Atoms' (57–73), 'What Will Be, Will Be' (74–100), 'There is Nothing' (101–7) and 'Let Us Seize the Moment' (108–43). Furughi and Ghani printed their selection in the manner traditional for collections of Persian poems: arranged, regardless of content, according to the alphabetical order of the last letter of each rhyming word.

The Ruba'iyat of Omar Khayyam

1   *Although I have a handsome face and colour,*
     Cheek like the tulips, form like the cypress,
     It is not clear why the Eternal Painter
     Thus tricked me out for the dusty show-booth of earth.

2   *He began my creation with constraint,*
     By giving me life he added only confusion;
     We depart reluctantly still not knowing
     The aim of birth, existence, departure.

3   *Heaven's wheel gained nothing from my coming,*
     Nor did my going augment its dignity;
     Nor did my ears hear from anyone
     Why I had to come and why I went.

4   *Oh heart you will not arrive at the solving of the riddle,*
     You will not reach the goal the wise in their subtlety seek;
     Make do here with wine and the cup of bliss,
     For you may and you may not arrive at bliss hereafter.

5   *If the heart could grasp the meaning of life,*
     In death it would know the mystery of God;
     Today when you are in possession of yourself, you know nothing.
     Tomorrow when you leave yourself behind, what will you know?

6*   *How long shall I lay bricks on the face of the seas?*
     I am sick of idolaters and the temple.
     Khayyam, who said that there will be a hell?
     Who's been to hell, who's been to heaven?

7   *Neither you nor I know the mysteries of eternity,*
          Neither you nor I read this enigma;
          You and I only talk this side of the veil;
          When the veil falls, neither you nor I will be here.

8   *This ocean of being has come from the Obscure,*
          No one has pierced this jewel of reality;
          Each has spoken according to his humour,
          No one can define the face of things.

9   *The bodies that occupy the celestial vault,*
          These give rise to wise men's uncertainties;
          Take care not to lose your grip on the thread of wisdom,
          Since the Powers That Be themselves are in a spin.

10   *The cycle which includes our coming and going*
          Has no discernible beginning nor end;
          Nobody has got this matter straight –
          Where we come from and where we go to.

11   *Since the Upholder embellishes the material of things,*
          For what reason does He cast it into diminution and decay?
          If it turned out good, why break it?
          If the form turned out bad, whose fault was it?

12   *Those who dominated the circle of learning and culture –*
          In the company of the perfect became lamps among their peers,
          By daylight they could not escape from the darkness,
          So they told a fable, and went to sleep.

13* *Those, boy, who went before*
  Have been laid in the dust of self-delusion;
  Go, drink wine and hear the truth from me,
  It was all hot air that they spoke.

14* *The uninformed who pierced the pearl of meaning,*
  Spoke concerning the wheel with a variety of opinions;
  Not encompassing the secrets of the world,
  They first bragged and then lay silent.

15 *A bull is next to the Pleiades in the sky,*
  Another bull is hidden below the earth;[1]
  If you're not blind, open your eyes to the truth,
  Below and above the two bulls is a drove of donkeys!

16 *Today is the time of my youth,*
  I drink wine because it is my solace;
  Do not blame me, although bitter it is pleasant,
  It is bitter because it is my life.

17 *If my coming here were my will, I would not have come,*
  Also, if my departure were my will, how should I go?
  Nothing could be better in this ruined lodging,
  Than not to have come, not to be, not to go.

1. An allusion to the ancient belief that the world is supported on the horns of a bull.

18 *What is the gain of our coming and going?*
 Where is the weft of our life's warp?
 In the circle of the spheres the lives of so many good men
 Burn and become dust, but where is the smoke?

19 *The pity of it that we should be shrivelled away,*
 To be cut down by the sickle of the spheres;
 Ah the pity, ah the sorrow – in the twinkling of an eye,
 Our desires unassuaged, we are blotted out.

20* *Though you may have lain with a mistress all your life,*
 Tasted the sweets of the world all your life;
 Still the end of the affair will be your departure –
 It was a dream that you dreamed all your life.

21 *Now when only the name of happiness is left,*
 No ripe comrade remaining but the rough wine,
 Keep the happy hand clenched to the wine-jug,
 Today when the jug is all the hand has got.

22 *If only there were occasion for repose,*
 If only this long road had an end,
 And in the track of a hundred thousand years, out of the heart of dust
 Hope sprang again, like greenness.

23 *Since all a man gets in this place of two doors*
 Is only a heart of sorrow and the giving up of life,
 He who never lived a moment is happy –
 That man is at peace whose mother never bore him.

24*   *Whoever set up earth and the wheel of the firmament,*
Branded so many hearts with sorrow,
Many a ruby lip and musk-scented tress
He put on this drum of earth and in this coffer of dust.

25   *If the firmament were in my hand as in God's,*
I would have razed it from the midst:
I would have made another firmament such that
The free of heart might easily attain their desire.

26   *The characters of all creatures are on the Tablet,*
The Pen always worn with writing 'Good', 'Bad':
Our grieving and striving are in vain,
Before time began all that was necessary was given.

27   *Since a day or a life cannot be lengthened or shortened,*
We should not distress ourselves with the more and the less;
It cannot be that your affairs and mine
Are shaped as we would judge, wax in our own hands.

28   *As the stars have no increase but sorrow,*
They restore nothing without taking away again;
If the unborn could know what we
Suffer from the universe, they would not come at all.

اجل هیاید این زندگی ها؟ | وزین هایهٔ زندگی که شرمند کی باد

چو سال نظارا رازده فزونش | لوای طاقت از هر سکون شد

به جوم شوق بر دل پا بفشرد | شکیب اندر لگکو که به هوس مرد

چو از آغوش شوق تاین شلهٔ زند | پسرین یغف بر کوش میرزد

که بر من مک شد مخواب و چشم | سکیم طاقت کشت از فرق حفت

یحیم

29 *You who are the product of the four elements and seven planets[2]*
 And because of that Four and this Seven in perpetual agitation,
 Drink wine; I have told you more than a thousand times
 There is no coming back for you, when you're gone, you're gone.

30* *While my dust was being tempered in the mould,*
 The dust of much trouble was raised;
 I cannot be better than I am –
 I am as I was poured from the crucible.

31* *How long will you talk of the mosque lamp and fire-temple smoke?*
 How long of hell's loss and heaven's profit?
 Go, see on the Tablet how the Master of Fate
 Has written what will be, before time began.

32* *Oh heart, since the world's reality is illusion,*
 How long will you complain about this torment?
 Resign your body to fate and put up with pain,
 Because what the Pen has written for you it will not unwrite.

2. Following Ptolemy, the Muslims held that there are seven 'wandering stars',
the planets – first the Moon, then Mercury, Venus, Sun, Mars, Jupiter, Saturn, each
in its own sphere – with Earth at the centre, the seven stars revolving round it.
The four elements are fire, air, water and earth, from which all creation, animal,
vegetable and mineral, is produced.

33   *The firmament secretly whispered in my heart,*
'Do you know what sentence fate laid on me?
If my revolving were in my control,
I would release myself from this circling.'

34   *The good and evil that are in man's heart,*
The joy and sorrow that are our fortune and destiny,
Do not impute them to the wheel of heaven because,
    in the light of reason,
The wheel is a thousand times more helpless than you.

35   *Alas, the book of youth is finished,*
The fresh spring of life has become winter;
That state which they call youth,
It is not perceptible when it began and when it closed.

36   *What a grief that our capital should have been exhausted,*
At the foot of doom many a heart lies broken;
No one has returned from that world for us to ask him
How the travellers of this world fare there.

37   *When we were children we went to the Master for a time,*
For a time we were beguiled with our own mastery;
Hear the end of the matter, what befell us:
We came like water and we went like wind.

38 *Convivial friends have all gone,*
    Death has trampled them down one after another;
    We were in one wine-bout at life's party,
    They got drunk a round or so ahead of us.

39 *Oh wheel of heaven, destruction comes from your malice,*
    Practising injustice is your ancient trade;
    Woe to earth if your breast were split open –
    What a precious stone indeed must lie there!

40 *Since the wheel turns at no wise man's will,*
    No matter if you count the spheres seven or eight;[3]
    Since we must die and all desires vanish,
    No matter whether the ant feeds in the grave,
       or the wolf above ground.

41 *There was a water-drop, it joined the sea,*
    A speck of dust, it was fused with earth;
    What of your entering and leaving this world?
    A fly appeared, and disappeared.

42* *You asked, 'What is this transient pattern?'*
    If we tell the truth of it, it will be a long story;
    It is a pattern that came up out of an ocean
    And in a moment returned to that ocean's depth.

3. See the note on Quatrain 29 above. The seven spheres are those
of the planets, but the question remained whether the so-called fixed stars
were to be considered as situated in an eighth sphere.

43   *It is a bowl the Creative Reason casts,*
Pressing in tenderness a hundred kisses on its brim;
This cosmic potter makes such a rare bowl,
Then throws it back again to the ground.

44   *The parts of a cup which are joined together*
The drunkard does not hold it lawful to break:
So many delicate heads, legs, hands,
Through whose love were they joined, by whose hatred smashed?

45   *Though the world is tricked out for you*
Do not make for what the wise shun:
Many like you come and many go,
Snatch your share before you are snatched away.

46   *Of all who went on this long road,*
Where is the one who has returned to tell us the secret?
Take care to leave nothing for your needs on this two-ended way,
You will not be coming back.

47   *Drink wine, you will lie long enough under the ground,*
Without companion, friend or comrade.
Take care you tell no one this hidden secret,
'No lily that withers will bloom again.'

48*   *I saw an old man in the wine-shop,*
I said, 'Have you any news of those who have gone?'
He replied, 'Take some wine, because like us many
Have gone, none has come back.'

49 *Much have I wandered about far and wide,*
  I have wandered as far as every horizon;
  I have heard of nobody who came from this road,
  The road he went by, the road of no return.

50 *We are the puppets and the firmament is the puppet-master,*
  In actual fact and not as a metaphor;
  For a time we acted on this stage,
  We went back one by one into the box of oblivion.

51 *Oh what a long time we shall not be and the world will endure,*
  Neither name nor sign of us will exist;
  Before this we were not and there was no deficiency,
  After this, when we are not it will be the same as before.

52 *On the surface of the earth I see only sleepers,*
  Under the earth I see those put away:
  The more I scan the void of oblivion,
  I only see the departed and the unborn.

53 *This is an old inn whose name is 'The World',*
  It is the piebald resthouse of night and day:
  It is the banquet of the left-overs of a hundred Jamshids,[4]
  The grave which is the bed-chamber of a hundred Bahrams.[5]

4. Jamshid was a legendary Persian king, the fourth in the mythical Pishdadian Dynasty, and the culture hero to whom many inventions and discoveries were attributed.

5. Bahram was the historical Bahram V (A.D. 420–38) of the Sasanid Dynasty, about whom legends have grown up, especially in connection with his love of hunting the wild ass, in Persian *gur*, a word which also means 'grave', so that the original contains a pun on this word. Bahram's favourite pursuit gained him the style 'Bahram-i-Gur', 'Bahram the Wild Ass'.

54 *That palace where Bahram took the cup in hand*
The antelope has made its couching-place and the fox its earth:
Bahram who hunted the wild ass all his life,
See how the grave has hunted him down.

55 *I saw a bird alighted on the city-walls of Tus[6]*
Grasping in its claws Kaika'us's[7] head:
It was saying to that head, 'Shame! Shame!
Where now the sound of the bells and the boom of the drum?'

56 *That place which once vied with heaven,*
Whose threshold kings touched with their foreheads;
We saw on its battlements a ring-dove
Perched, saying: 'Coo? Coo? Where? Where?'[8]

57 *When your dear soul and mine have left the body,*
They will set on our graves two tiles;
And then, for the tiles on others' graves,
They will set your dust and mine in a mould.

6. An ancient city in Khurasan, gradually supplanted in importance by the nearby city of Meshed.

7. A king of the legendary Kayani Dynasty. The reference to 'bells' underlines the evocation of pagan or pre-Islamic times; the use of bells, associated with Christians, non-believers in the eyes of Muslims, was forbidden in Islamic countries.

8. The poet plays on the ring-dove's 'coo' and the Persian interrogative *ku*, meaning 'where?'; in the original the *ku, ku* is repeated four times.

58*   *Every particle of dust on a patch of earth*
Was a sun-cheek or brow of the morning star;
Shake the dust off your sleeve carefully –
That too was a delicate, fair face.

59   *Oh wise elder, get up earlier in the morning,*
Look closely at that boy sifting dust;
Advise him, 'Gently, gently sift
The brains of Kaikobad[9] and eyes of Parviz.'[10]

60   *Look, the morning breeze has torn the rose's dress,*
The nightingale is in ecstasy at the rose's beauty;
Sit in the rose's shade, for many such
Have come from earth and to it returned.

61   *The cloud came and wept on the greenness,*
Oh rose-hued wine, there is no living without you;
This green is our pleasure-ground today,
But whose pleasure-ground will be the green springing from our dust?

62   *When the cloud washes the tulip's cheek at New Year,[11]*
Get up and make firmly for the wine-cup,
Because this green spot that today is your pleasure-ground
Tomorrow will all be growing out of your dust.

9. Another legendary king of the Kayani Dynasty, served by the champion Rustam.

10. Parviz may be taken as a 'historical' reference – Khosrau Parviz of the Sasanid Dynasty ruled as King of Kings in Persia from A.D. 590 to 628. He is celebrated for his patronage of poetry and of the famous poet Barbad, and for his steed, Shabdiz.

11. The Persian New Year is at the Vernal Equinox.

63   *All the plants that grow beside the stream*
Have surely grown from angels' lips;
Tread roughly on no plant,
For it has sprung out of the dust of the tulip-cheeked.

64   *Drink wine since for our destruction*
The firmament has got its eye on our precious souls;
Sit where it is green and enjoy the sparkling liquor,
Because this grass will grow nicely from your dust and mine.

65*   *I saw a man working on a building site,*
He was stamping down the clay;
The clay protested,
'Stop it, you like me will be stamped on by many a foot.'

66   *Oh heart-seeker raise the cup and the jug,*
Go back to the meadows on the stream's verge:
This wheel has made many a radiant-cheeked, idol-form
Over and over again into cups and jugs.

67   *Last night I smashed an earthenware pot on the stones,*
I was drunk when I committed this folly:
The pot protested,
'I was like you, you will be like me also.'

68   *From that wine-jug which has no harm in it,*
Fill a bowl, boy, drink and pass it to me,
Before, by some wayside,
A potter uses your clay and mine for just such a jug.

69*   *I passed by a potter the day before last,*
He was ceaselessly plying his skill with the clay,
And, what the blind do not see, I could –
My father's clay in every potter's hand.

70*   *Stop, potter, if you have any sense,*
How long will you debase man's clay?
You have put Feridun's[12] finger and Kaikhosrau's[13] hand
On the wheel – what do you think you're doing?

71   *I watched a potter in his work-place,*
Saw the master, his foot on the wheel's treddle;
Unabashed, he was making a jug's lid and handle
From a king's head and a beggar's hand.

72   *This jug was love-sick like me,*
Tangled in a fair girl's locks;
This handle you now see on its neck
Was his hand on the neck of the girl.

73   *I was in the potter's shop last night,*
And saw two thousand jugs, some speaking, some dumb;
Each was anxiously asking,
'Where is the potter, and the buyer and seller of pots?'

12. The legendary king who defeated a usurper to restore the golden age of Jamshid.
13. A king of the legendary Kayani Dynasty.

74   *If I'm drunk on forbidden wine,*[14] *so I am!*
And if I'm an unbeliever, a pagan or idolater, so I am!
Every sect has its own suspicions of me,
I myself am just what I am.

75   *My rule of life is to drink and be merry,*
To be free from belief and unbelief is my religion:
I asked the Bride of Destiny her bride-price,
'Your joyous heart,' she said.

76   *I cannot live without the sparkling vintage,*
Cannot bear the body's burden without wine:
I am a slave to that last gasp when the wine-server says,
'Have another,' and I can't.

77   *Tonight I will make a tun of wine,*
Set myself up with two bowls of it;
First I will divorce absolutely reason and religion,
Then take to wife the daughter of the vine.

78*   *When I am dead, scatter my dust*
And make my condition an example to men:
Moisten my dust with wine,
To make the seal on a vat out of my corpse.

14. The original has 'Magian wine', i.e., that of the cult of the Magi,
an alternative name for Zoroastrian priests, implying the ancient religion of Persia
– or any other ancient Near Eastern non-Islamic faith which, unlike Islam,
permitted wine.

79* *Wash me in wine when I go,* [15]
     For my burial service use a text concerning wine;
     Would you find me on the Day of Doom,
     Look for me in the dust at the wine-shop's door.

80* *I drink so much wine, its aroma*
     Will rise from the dust when I'm under it;
     Should a toper come upon my dust,
     The fragrance from my corpse will make him roaring drunk.

81   *The day when my life's branch is uprooted*
     And my members are dispersed,
     Should my clay be used to make a cup
     It would come to life as soon as it was filled with wine.

82* *When I am prostrate at the feet of doom,*
     My hope of life torn up by the root,
     Take care to use my clay only for a goblet –
     The smell of wine might restore me life for a moment.

83* *When you are in convivial company,*
     You must remember ardently your friend:
     When you are drinking mellow wine together
     And my turn comes, invert the glass.

15. This line echoes one in an ode to wine by the poet Minuchihri (died 1040)
'Oh my noble friends, when I die, wash my body in the reddest of wine

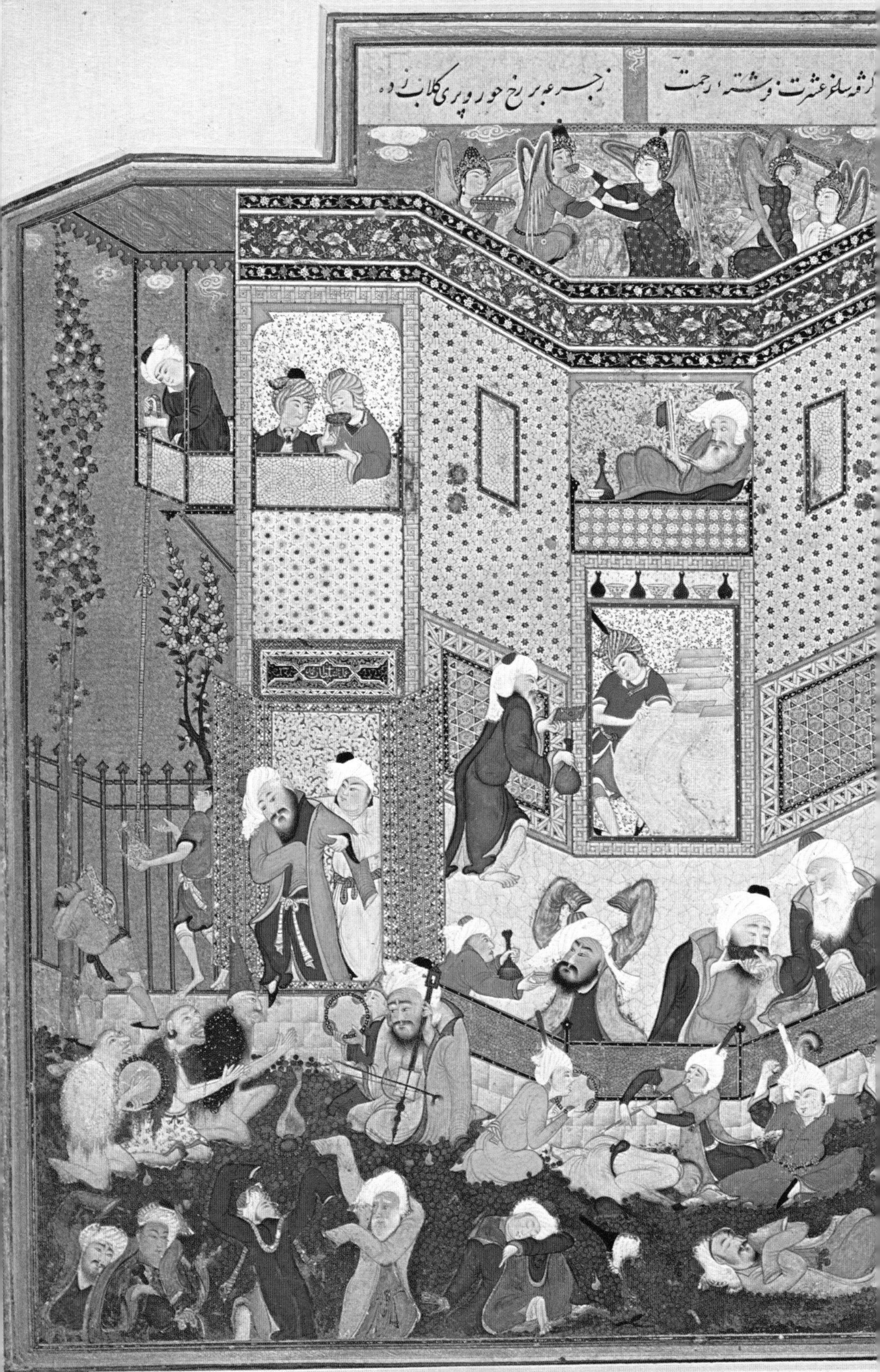
ساغر عشرت فرشته رحمت
ز جرعه بر رخ حور و پری گلاب زده

84* The captives of intellect and of the nice distinction,
     Worrying about Being and Non-Being themselves
         become nothing;[16]
     You with the news, go and seek out the juice of the vine,
     Those without it wither before they're ripe.

85* Oh Canon Jurist,[17] we work better than you,
     With all this drunkenness, we're more sober:
     You drink men's blood, we, the vine's,
     Be honest – which of us is the more bloodthirsty?

86   A religious man said to a whore, 'You're drunk,
     Caught every moment in a different snare.'
     She replied, 'Oh Shaikh, I am what you say,
     Are you what you seem?'

87* They say lovers and drunkards go to hell,
     A controversial dictum not easy to accept:
     If the lover and drunkard are for hell,
     Tomorrow Paradise will be empty.

16. One of the major paradoxes in ancient thought lay in the question
of the Being of the finite ideal Forms of Plato in relation to the One, the infinite
'Being' from which, as urged by Plotinus, who developed Plato's themes five
centuries after him, all else springs. Since Being is finite, the One, the infinite
Unity, is beyond Being: the Non-Being in which all Being has its ground.
     17. Literally, 'Lord of the Judicial Decree'. These decrees, *fatwas*, were issued
according to interpretations of Muslim Law which the Caliph, Mufti or Qazi (Judge)
was empowered to give. They generally took a syllogistic or question-and-answer
form, and were the sentences, given in writing, by which the law was executed and
acts validated or nullified.

88 *They promise there will be Paradise and the houri-eyed,*
    Where clear wine and honey will flow:
    Should we prefer wine and a lover, what's the harm?
    Are not these the final recompense?

89* *They say there is Paradise with the houris and the River,* [18]
    Wine freshets, milk, sweets and honey:
    Fill the wine-cup, put it in my hand —
    Cash is better than a thousand promises.

90* *They say houris make the gardens of Paradise delicious,*
    I say that the juice of the vine is delicious,
    Take this cash and reject that credit —
    The sound of a distant drum, brother, is sweet.

91 *Nobody, heart, has seen heaven or hell,*
    Tell me, dear, who has returned from there?
    Our hopes and fears are on something of which,
    My dear, there is no indication but the name.

92* *I do not know whether he who shaped me*
    Made me for heaven or grim hell:
    A cup, a lover and music on the field's verge —
    These three are my cash, heaven your I.O.U.

18. The Paradise of the *Koran* contains beautiful girls – the houris – wine, honey, etc., and a river, the source of all the other streams that freshen Paradise.

93 *Since in this sphere we have no abiding place,*
To be without wine and a lover is a mistake:
How long shall hopes and fears persist whether the world
 is created or eternal?[19]
When I am gone, created and eternal worlds are the same.

94 *Since at first my coming was not at my will,*
And the going is involuntarily imposed,
Arise, fasten your belt brisk wine-boy,
I'll drown the world's sorrow in wine.

95 *When life comes to an end it will be the same*
 in Baghdad or Balkh,[20]
When the cup brims over, it is the same if sweet or bitter:
Be glad, because after our time many a moon
Will grow full, and then wane.

96* *Go only the way of tavern-roisterers,*
Seek for girls, wine and music:
Wine-cup in hand, the wine-skin on the shoulder,
Drink the wine, my darling, and stop chattering.

19. The reference is to the dictum of Aristotle's neo-Platonic commentators, that the world being coeval with the Unmovable Mover cannot have been created but must be eternal or 'continuous' with the One beyond Being.

20. Balkh, in what is today north Afghanistan, was in Khayyam's time the easternmost city in Khurasan, the north-eastern province of Persia. Baghdad was in the south-west, at the other end of the Eastern Caliphate.

97* *Boy, my longing has become clamorous,*
  My drunkenness goes beyond all bounds:
  My grey-haired head is besotted – by your wine
  An old man's heart is once more spring.

98* *I need a jug of wine and a book of poetry,*
  Half a loaf for a bite to eat,
  Then you and I, seated in a deserted spot,
  Will have more wealth than a Sultan's realm.

99* *I know Being and Non-Being's outward form,*
  I know every exaltation and depression's inwardness:
  With all this knowledge, may I be ashamed
  To know any stage beyond drunkenness.

100 *I still have a breath left, thanks to the wine-boy's care,*
  But of consorting with men only their ingratitude remains:
  No more than one cup of last night's wine is left,
  But of life I don't know how much more there is.

101 *Oh you without knowledge, the corporeal shape is nothing,*
  And this dome of the nine charted spheres is nothing:[21]
  Take comfort, in the place of being and decay
  We are creatures of a single moment – also nothing.

21. In the Nine the poet includes the seven planets, the fixed stars and the Aristotelian *Primum Mobile*. (See note on Quatrain 29.)

102   *You have seen the world and all you saw was nothing,*
All you have said and heard, that too is nothing:
Running from pole to pole, there was nothing,
And when you lurked at home, there was also nothing.

103   *Suppose the world went as you wanted, then what?*
And suppose this book of life were read through, then what?
Let me suppose a century of self-gratification left,
Even supposing we had a century more, then what?

104*   *I saw a waster sitting on a patch of ground,*
Heedless of belief and unbelief, the world and the faith –
No God, no Truth, no Divine Law, no Certitude:
Who in either of the worlds has the courage of this man?

105   *Let us consider this wheel of heaven that amazes us,*
As if it were a diorama –
The sun the candle, the world the lanthorn,
Then we are like the images revolving on its walls.

106   *Since all that is leaves us empty-handed,*
The only return from all that is, loss and ruin,
It can be supposed that what the world has not, is,
And what it has, is not.

107   *See what I've got from the world, nothing;*
The fruit of my life's work? Nothing:
I am the light of the party, but when I sit down, I am nothing;
I am a wine-pot, but when I'm broken, nothing.

108   *It is a flash from the stage of non-belief to faith,*
There is no more than a syllable between doubt and certainty:
Prize this precious moment dearly,
It is our life's only fruit.

109   *Go for pleasure, life only gives a moment,*
Its every atom from a Kaikobad's or a Jamshid's dust;
The world's phenomena and life's essence
Are all a dream, a fancy, and a moment's deception.

110   *Nobody has known anything better than sparkling wine*
Since the morning star and the moon graced the sky:
Wine-sellers astonish me because
What can they buy better than what they sell?

111   *The moonbeam splinters night's skirt with light –*
Drink wine, there is no better time than this:
Be glad, but remember how long for moonbeams
There'll only be your grave and mine to shine on.

112   *Since nobody has a lien on tomorrow*
Gladden the sad heart now:
Drink wine in the moonlight, my dear,
Because the moon will revolve a long time and not find us.

113   *The year's caravan goes by swiftly,*
Seize the cheerful moment:
Why sorrow, boy, over tomorrow's grief for friends?
Bring out the cup – the night passes.

76

114   *Do you know why the cock crows*
So early in the whiteness of dawn?
He tells that the morning's mirror shows
One more night of life gone, and you heedless.

115   *Get up my sweetest, it is dawn,*
Gently, gently sip the wine and twang the harp,
For not a soul will remain of those here,
And of those gone, none will return.

116   *Happy sweetheart, at dawn*
Sing a snatch and bring out the wine:
A legion of Kais[22] and Jamshids have turned to dust,
But summer's on the way and winter is passed.

117   *It is morning, let us pour out the rose-red wine,*
Smashing on the rocks the glass of fame and reputation:
Let us draw back from much projected hopes,
Turning towards long tresses and the strings of the harp.

118   *A nice day, neither too hot nor cold,*
Clouds sprinkling the dust from cheeks that were rose-gardens:
The nightingale in the old tongue of Persia cries out
To the yellow rose, 'Wine is for wassail.'[23]

22. Ancient kings of the Kayani Dynasty of legendary fame.

23. The word 'wassail' is used here as being from the Old English *wæs*, 'be thou' and *hal*, 'whole' (a form of salutation), because in the original the nightingale's command. 'Drink . . .', is cleverly stated in an archaic form. The climatic reference is echoed by the great Persian poet Hafiz (died A.D. 1390) when he begins a line in one of his lyrics about springtime with the words: 'The air is good, giving joy . . .'

130*   *Come friend, let us lose tomorrow's grief*
And seize this moment of life:
Tomorrow, this ancient inn abandoned,
We shall be equal with those born seven thousand years ago!

131*   *Be silent, you are beneath unscrupulous stars,*
Drink wine, you are in a world of calamities:
Since your beginning and end are only of dust,
Do not imagine you are on the earth, but in it.

132*   *Put wine into my hand, my heart is tormented,*
And fleet-footed life is like quicksilver;
Beware, the fire of youth is water!
Watch, fortune's waking is sleep![25]

133   *Drink wine, this is life eternal,*
This, all that youth will give you:
It is the season for wine, roses and friends drinking together,
Be happy for this moment – it is all life is.

134   *Make wine your intimate, it is Mahmud's kingdom,*[26]
And listen to the harp, it is King David's psalmody:
Forget those who have been and gone,
Make the present happy, this is the aim.

25. Good fortune is thought of as awake, vigilant; when it is not, a man is deprived of luck.

26. Mahmud of Ghazna ruled an empire in north-eastern Persia and what is today Afghanistan between A.D. 998 and 1030. He occurs elsewhere in Sufi poetry as a kind of paragon.

گفت ای یار و سپت از دامنم مدار که بار ما دریں مصلحت که توبی هنپے اندکیذیم

135   *Today, tomorrow is not within your reach,*
        To think of it is only morbid:
        If the heart is awake, do not waste this moment —
        There is no proof of life's continuance.

136*   *The world's gyrations without wine and its server are pointless,*
        Nothing without the wail of an Iraqi flute;[27]
        The more I look at the world's condition,
        To be convivial is the answer, the rest nothing.

137   *How long shall I grieve for what I have or have not,*
        Over whether to pass my life in pleasure?
        Fill the wine-bowl — it is not certain
        That I shall breathe out again the breath I now draw.

138   *If we don't clap hands together as one,*
        We cannot tread down sorrow with our feet in joy:
        Let us go on and be happy before the breath of dawn —
        Many a day will break when we breathe no more.

139   *In the extremity of desire I put my lip to the pot's*
        To seek the elixir of life:
        It put its lip on mine and murmured,
        'Enjoy the wine, you'll not be here again.'

27. Iraq was the area measured from Abadan on the Persian Gulf to Mosul in present-day Iraq and from the region in western Persia near Kirmanshah to the district south of the River Euphrates, while 'Persian Iraq' – '*Iraq-i-'Ajam* – comprised the western part of central Persia south of the Alborz Mountains.

140   *Khayyam, if you are drunk on wine, enjoy it,*
If you are with the tulip-cheeked, enjoy her:
Since the world's business ends in nothing,
Think that you are not and, while you are, enjoy it.

141   *Tomorrow I will haul down the flag of hypocrisy,*
I will devote my grey hairs to wine:
My life's span has reached seventy,
If I don't enjoy myself now, when shall I?

142   *The globe is the image of a ball compacted of our bones,*
The Oxus, a trickle of our distilled tears;
Hell is a spark from our consuming torments,
Paradise, a moment from our space of reprieve.

143   *How long will you live in self-love,*
Or run after Being and Non-Being?
Drink wine, a life so dogged by sorrow
Is best spent in sleep or drunkenness.

*

144   *Rise up my love and solve our problem by your beauty,*
Bring a jug of wine to clear our heart
So that we may drink together
Before wine-jugs are made of our clay.

145   *They call the Koran the Ultimate Word,*
They read it occasionally but not all the time;
A text stands round the inside of the cup,[28]
This they con at all times and in all places.

146   *Although you do not drink wine, don't be hard on topers,*
Don't lay snares to catch them out;
Don't boast of not drinking —
You devour many a morsel to which wine is a mere subsidiary.

147   *Here we are with wine, music and this broken-down corner,*
Heart, soul, the cup, clothes stained with wine-dregs,
Void of hope of mercy and fear of punishment,
Free from earth, air, fire and water.

148   *Now that your flower of happiness has come to fruition,*
Why is your hand not occupied with the wine-cup?
Drink wine because Time is a treacherous enemy,
Coming upon such a day as this is not easy.

28. Persian wine bowls often had a line of verse engraved round the inside rim, but this could also refer to the magic cup of Jamshid, by which all time and the world were revealed to him. The conceit speaks of pre-Islamic pleasures and powers of divination.

149 *Oh you come hot-foot from the spiritual world,*
Distracted by the five senses, four elements, six causes
  and seven planets;
Drink wine since you do not know where you're from,
Be happy, you do not know where you will go.

150 *Oh heart since time's passing grieves you*
And your pure spirit so unseasonably leaves the body,
Sit on the green, spend a few days in happiness
Before the green grass springs from your dust.

151 *This pot a workman drinks from*
Is made from the eyes of a king, the heart of a vazir;
This wine-bowl in a drunkard's palm
Is made from a cheek flushed with wine and a lady's lip.

152 *These few odd days of life have passed*
Like water down the brook, wind across the desert;
There are two days I have never been plagued with regret for,
Yesterday that has gone, tomorrow that will come.

153 *Before you and I did, night and day existed,*
The revolving heavens were busy;
Where you set your foot on the face of the ground
Was the pupil of the eye of a sweetheart.

154   *When the conjunctions of matter are working in your favour*
          a moment
    Go and live happily, you did not choose your lot;
    Keep company with men of science since your bodily properties
    Are a speck of dust joined with a puff of air,
          a mote with a gasp of breath.

155   *When the drunken nightingale found his way into the garden*
    He discovered the face of the rose and the wine-cup laughing;
    He came to whisper in my ear excitedly,
    'Seek out these, life once gone cannot be sought again.'

156   *Since neither truth nor certainty is granted*
    You cannot sit in doubtful hope all your life;
    Let us be careful not to set the wine-cup aside,
    Since a man is in ignorance, drunk or sober.

157   *The dust under every fool's foot*
    Is a darling's upturned hand and a sweetheart's cheek;
    Every brick that tops an arch
    Is the finger of a vazir or a royal head.

158   *No one knows the way through the curtain of mysteries,*
    No one's soul has true knowledge of this natural life,
    There is no resting-place but in the heart of earth,
    Drink wine because these tales are never finished.

159   *I was asleep, a wise man said to me*
'The rose of joy does not bloom for slumberers;
Why are you asleep? Sleep is the image of death,
Drink wine, below the ground you must sleep of necessity.'

160   *In spring if a houri-like sweetheart*
Gives me a cup of wine on the edge of a green cornfield,
Though to the vulgar this would be blasphemy,
If I mentioned any other Paradise, I'd be worse than a dog.

161   *Know for a certainty that you'll be separated from the soul,*
You'll go behind the curtain of the mysteries of extinction;
Drink wine – you don't know where you have come from,
Be happy – you don't know where you will go to.

162   *I live a life that is overcast, all my affairs are in a tangle,*
Disasters increase, ease decreases;
God be thanked that for what causes our troubles
He alone is answerable to us.

163   *Though the five cords of fortune support your prop of stability*
And on your body life is a fine garment,
In the tent of the body which is your shelter
Don't be secure, its four pegs are unstable.[29]

29. The four tent-pegs which support the body's tent are the four humours, bodily fluids corresponding to the four elements. It was believed that health depended on a proper balance of these four humours to give a 'good-tempered' man.

164   *Wine is liquid ruby, the flask the mine,*
The cup is the body, its wine the soul;
That crystal goblet laughing with wine
Is a tear, the heart's blood hidden inside it.

165   *Every plain where tulips bloomed*
Was reddened by a prince's blood;
Every knot of violets springing from the earth
Was a beauty-patch on a darling's cheek.

166   *A draught of wine is better than Ka'us's kingdom*
And the throne of Qubad,[30] the old realm of Tus;
Every groan a waster heaves up at dawn
Is better than a hypocrite devotee's litany.

167   *What was sported with on the field of Causality[31]*
Was not there when the rules of the game were laid down;
It was thrown in today by way of pretext,
Tomorrow all will be as was set up before.

168   *Those who have grown old and these who are young,*
Each runs his course at his own desire;
This old world is not permanent for anyone,
They have gone and we shall go also, others will come
      and they will go, too.

30. Qubad, Kay Qubad, father and predecessor of Kay Ka'us, who is mentioned in the preceding line.

31. A conceit based on the game of polo or mall. The life of a man is likened to a ball driven hither and thither by those forces which rule the universe.

169   *One is fetched out and another snatched away,*
The secret of being is not disclosed to anyone;
By destiny only this amount is allotted to us,
The brief measure of our lifetime.

170   *Suffering ennobles a man,*
Enduring the oyster-shell's prison makes a pearl of a water-drop;
Though worldly goods perish let your head remain like a cup –
When the cup is empty it may be filled again.

171   *This reason which seeks the way of bliss*
Says again and again to you,
'Seize this moment which is yours:
You are not that herb which is cut down only to flourish anew.'

172   *My back is bent by time,*
All my affairs go awry;
Life was ready to depart. I said, 'Don't go.'
It replied, 'What else can I do, if the house is falling down?'

173   *Nobody has mastered the wheel of the firmament,*
Earth is never glutted feeding on men;
You boast it has not eaten you,
Don't speak too soon, it's early yet, it will.

174   *The Pen of Destiny is made to write my record without me,*
Why are its good and bad accounted to me
Yesterday without me, and today likewise with neither you nor me?
Tomorrow on what evidence shall I be summoned before the Judge?

175   *How long will you be enthralled by colour and scent*
Running after the foul or the fair?
Though you be the fountain of Zamzam[32] or the Water of Life,
You will sink at last to the depths of the earth.

176   *Nothing is gained until you follow the path of one*
     in utter poverty;
Nothing is gained unless tears of blood wash your cheek;
Why enflame desire? Nothing is possible till you abandon selfhood
Freely, like the pure whose hearts are consumed away.

177   *The Living God who has the power to make skulls and faces*
Always botches his work;
They say a maker of wine-jars can be no good Muslim,
What is to be said of Him who makes the gourd?[33]

178   *When the world is filled with the rumour of the fresh rose*
Command, love, the wine to be copiously poured;
Don't bother about houris, heavenly mansions,
Paradise, Hell – they're all rumour, too.

179   *Anybody who in this world has half a loaf*
And a home in which to live
Is no man's master and no man's slave;
Say to him, 'Be happy always,' for he possesses a world
     of happiness.

32. The sacred well within the precincts of the mosque at Mecca.
33. The potter is condemned for making artificial wine-cups, but God made the gourd, a natural drinking vessel.

180   *The husbandman of destiny has sown and reaped many like us,*
Grieving is vain and brings no profit;
Fill the wine-cup and put it in my hand quickly
For me to drink again; since all that has to be has been.

181   *Before you are taken in ambush*
Order the rose-hued wine to be fetched;
You're not gold, you silly fool,
To be buried in the ground and then brought out again.

182   *Nobody has uncovered the difficulties of death's mysteries,*
Nor taken one step beyond what was decreed;
I survey all from tyros to masters,
Impotence is in the grasp of all born of woman.

183   *Do not expect much of the world and live contented,*
Ignore the good and ill that time brings;
Take wine in your hand and a sweet girl's tresses
For they quickly go and these few days do not last.

184   *My sorrows and pain make a long story*
But your liveliness and joy can rise above them;
Don't rely on either, the turns of the firmament
Have a thousand varieties of show behind the curtain.

185   *The skies' vault only brings flowers out of earth*
To crush them and consign them to earth again;
If the clouds took up dust as they do water,
They would rain till Doomsday the blood of those we have loved.

186   *When a moment of life goes by*
Let it only pass in joy;
Be careful, for the stock-in-trade of this world's market
Is the life you purchase for yourself.

187   *They say all those who cultivate abstinence*
Are resurrected like the men they died;[34]
In that case we cultivate wine and girls all the time
To be awakened at the Resurrection the same as we were.

188   *Drink wine, it stops you thinking about the Many and the One,*[35]
Dispels thoughts about the seventy-two jarring sects;
Don't abstain, the physic you get
In one draught of it rids you of a thousand sicknesses.

189   *All the secrets a wise heart has*
Must be more hidden than the Phoenix is,
Because concealment in the oyster-shell makes the pearl
From that water-drop that comes from the depths of the ocean.

190   *Every morning when the dew washes the face of the tulip*
The violet's stem droops in the meadow;
But truly I prefer that bud which
Stands erect, its skirts drawn in unruffled.

34. According to Muslim belief, at the Resurrection the body will be raised as it was in life and reunited to the soul.

35. A reference to the controversy about whether God knew only Universals, or Particulars as well, which according to Aristotelians He could not know. This belief orthodox Muslim philosophers found repugnant.

191   *My mind has never lacked learning,*
           Few mysteries remain unconned;
           I have meditated for seventy-two years night and day,
           To learn that nothing has been learned at all.

192   *One grain of hope alone remains on the threshing floor,*
           Though the gardens and palaces will stay after you and I are gone:
           Spend all you have among friends from the pound to the penny,
           For if you don't it will be left for your enemies.

193   *One cup of wine is worth a hundred hearts and religions,*
           One sip worth the realm of China;
           Apart from ruby wine on the earth's expanse
           No other bitter thing exists worth thousands of sweet souls.

194   *If all a man gets in two days is one loaf*
           And a drop of cold water from a cracked pitcher,
           Why should you serve those less than you are?
           Why must you serve those who are your equals?

195   *Bring that ruby in a plain glass*
           And bring my boon companion and friend of the free;
           Since you know that the days of this world of dust
           Are a wind which quickly passes, fetch the wine.

196   *What have you to do with Being, friend,*
           And empty opinions about the notion of mind and spirit?
           Joyfully live and let the world pass happily,
           The beginning of the matter was not arranged with you in mind.

206   *Awake from sleep that we may have one drink of wine*
Before Time's brutal potion is handed to us,
Since the sudden turns of this tyrannical wheel
Do not leave enough time even for a sip of water.

207   *I will arise and betake myself to the bright wine*
Till I colour my cheeks red as a berry;
As I do in my dreams I will slap this officious reason
In the face with wine in hand.

208   *How long are we to be prisoners of workaday reason?*
What difference does it make if we're here a hundred years
    or one day?
Pour wine into the bowl before we are turned
Into wine-bowls in the potter's shop.

209   *I cannot hide what stands out a mile,*
I cannot tell the mysteries of Time;
My intellect dredges from thought's ocean
A pearl which I fear to thread.

210   *My enemy mistakenly calls me a philosopher,*[38]
God knows I'm not what he says;
But since I have come to this abode of sorrow
I am too insignificant to know what I am.

38. That is, the enemy of orthodox religion – a 'free-thinker'.

211 *It is we who are the source of our own happiness,*
   the mine of our own sorrow,
 The repository of justice and foundation of iniquity;
 We who are cast down and exalted, perfect and defective,
 At once the rusted mirror and Jamshid's all-seeing cup.[39]

212 *I drink no wine, but not because I'm poor,*
 Nor get drunk, though not through fear of scandal;
 I drank to lighten my heart
 But now that you have settled in my heart, I drink no more.

213 *Every now and then someone comes along saying, 'It is I.'*
 He arrives with favours, silver and gold, saying, 'It is I.'
 When his little affair is sorted out for a day,
 Death suddenly jumps out of ambush saying, 'It is I.'

214 *I am not free one single day from bondage to the world,*
 Get not one breath of joy from all my existence;
 I have served a long apprenticeship to Time
 But am still no master of this world's business.

215 *Don't seek to recall yesterday that is past*
 Nor repine for tomorrow which has not yet come;
 Don't build your hopes on the past or the future,
 Be happy now and don't live on wind.

39. To the Persian culture hero Jamshid or Jam was attributed a magic cup in which he could see time past, present and future and all the world, and by which, like Joseph with his silver cup, he could divine (*Genesis* xliv, 4–5).

216   *Oh eye you are not blind, see the grave*
And see this world full of distraction and bitterness;
Kings, heads and princes are under the clay,
See moon-bright faces in the jaws of ants.

217   *Since a man's gain in this salt marsh*
Is nothing till life's uprooting but misery,
He who leaves this world soon is happy of heart,
And he who never entered it at peace.

218   *Since in this halting-place there is no justice,*
And there will be nothing but empty air in the hand, I'm off!
Those alone who escape the grasp of death
Can rejoice at my death.

219   *To be content like a vulture with a bone*
Is better than being the uninvited guest at nobody's feast;
To be with your own barley bread is certainly better
Than to be polluted by the confections of nonentities.

220   *One lot cogitates on the way of religion,*
Another ponders on the path of mystical certainty;
But I fear one day the cry will go up,
'Oh you fools, neither this nor that is the way!'

221   Pay no heed to the tattle of time's servants,
      Call for wine strained by the gaily dressed wine-server;
      Those who came have departed one by one
      And there's no sign that any have returned.

222   Drinking wine and consorting with good fellows
      Is better than practising the ascetic's hypocrisy;
      If the lover and drunkard are to be among the damned
      Then no one will see the face of heaven.

223   Let not sorrow wither the joyful heart
      Nor stones of affliction wear away your season of happiness;
      Nobody knows the hidden future –
      Wine, a lover and enjoying the heart's desire are all you need.

224   Short measures are best of everything except wine
      And wine is best from the hand of courtly beauties;
      Drunkenness, no restraint, apostasy are best –
      Of all things between heaven and earth one draught of wine
          is best.

225   One draught of old wine is preferable to a new empire,
      It is best to get out of any way not the way of wine;
      The last of the wine is a hundred times better than Feridun's
          throne,
      The clay lid of a wine-vat better than Kaikhosrau's kingdom.

226   *These worldly goods which you need for use –*
It is permitted that you should strive to get them,
But laying up what you have not gained by your own efforts
    is worthless,
Beware lest you barter your days for that.

227   *I once bought a pot from a potter*
Which told everything when it said
'I was an emperor and had a golden goblet,
Now I'm any drunkard's wine-pot.'

228   *Friend, listen to what I have to tell of the truth,*
Stay with the red wine and a silver body;
Whoever made the world could not care less
About the pair of moustaches you are and the beard I am.

229   *Were I to find fruit on the branch of hope*
I'd find the end of my life's thread there;
How much longer must I be in existence's narrow straits?
If only I could find the door to oblivion.

230   *Take up the cup, dearest, and the jug,*
Sit at ease in the green field by the edge of the stream;
The vile wheel a hundred times over has made
Many dear ones into cups and jugs.

231   *How long boy will you chatter about the five senses*
        and the four elements?
    What matter if the puzzles be one or a hundred thousand?
    We are dust, strum the harp boy.
    We are air, boy, bring out the wine.

232   *For all that I look on every side,*
    In the garden flows a brook from the River of Paradise;
    Since this meadow is like enough Paradise talk less
        of the River of Paradise,
    Sit in your paradise with a heavenly-faced girl.

233   *Rest content, your passionate humour was concocted yesterday,*
    Yesterday all your lust was implanted;
    How can I recount that not at your asking
    Your tomorrow was fixed yesterday?

234   *If chance supplied a loaf of white bread,*
    Two casks of wine and a leg of mutton,
    In the corner of a garden with a tulip-cheeked girl
    There'd be enjoyment no Sultan could outdo.

235   *If the firmament's transactions had been weighed justly*
    All of its states would turn out to be agreeable;
    If there were any justice in the workings of the spheres
    How could the minds of men of discernment ever be afflicted?

Of authors whose contemporary or near-contemporary comments on Khayyam were mentioned in the *Introduction*, none associate him with the Isma'ili sect, whose lone assassins terrorized Persia during the Saljuq period. This sect sprang out of the Islamic faction called Shi'a, 'faction'. The Shi'a was Islam's second major division, opposed to the Sunnis, the orthodox majority. Conflict between the two divisions hinged on who should succeed the Prophet Muhammad as leader of the Muslim community. As he was the Seal of Prophecy, there was no question of succession to him as the vehicle of God's Revelation. But when Muhammad died his community needed a leader. He had no sons and the Sunnis claimed he had designated no one for this office, which should be open to whomever by general consent was considered of sufficient virtue and experience to lead the Muslim state as a *primus inter pares*.

The Shi'a opposition claimed that the Prophet had so obviously treated his son-in-law and cousin 'Ali as a favourite that even if he had not, as they claimed he had, declared that 'Ali should succeed him, 'Ali was nevertheless heir. 'Ali, the husband of the Prophet's favourite daughter Fatima, had lived in great intimacy with his father-in-law, but did not succeed him as the *Khalifa* (Caliph), or deputy, until three others had reigned with the consensus of the people. The Prophet died in 632, and 'Ali eventually became Caliph in 656. In 661 he was murdered and the Shi'is were left in opposition to the triumphant Sunnis. Though their legitimist principle had not won, neither had the elective principle – the Caliphate became vested in, first, the family of Umayya, which was ousted in 750 by the family of Al-'Abbas. The 'Abbasids moved the capital from Damascus to Baghdad, where they remained Caliphs until 1258, when Hulagu Khan the Mongol executed the last 'Abbasid Caliph.

Meanwhile, Shi'ism gained adherents among the people the Arabs had conquered and whose ancient institutional ideas found a response in the Shi'i belief that only heirs of the Prophet through his daughter and her husband should be the Imams, the guides of the Muslim community. Also, their ancient religious and cult practices encouraged the notion that the Prophet must have given 'Ali special spiritual gifts: he and his descendants seemed the only legitimate Imams on grounds other than the purely secular. Shi'ism attracted deprived or oppressed people, who found the Arabs and their supporters inimical. It became a banner of discontent.

The Shi'i faction itself split. Ja'far as-Sadiq was the sixth Shi'i Imam in descent from 'Ali. When he died in 765, his eldest son Isma'il was passed over for the succession because of alleged drunkenness and lack of leadership. One party preferred his brother Musa al-Kazim. Another thought Ja'far as-Sadiq immortal, to return as the expected Mahdi, the Shi'i Messiah, so the question of a successor did not arise. A third party favoured Isma'il.

The Isma'ilis developed into a powerful underground movement and ultimately established the Fatimid Caliphs in Egypt, who survived from 909 until 1171 and opposed the Caliphs of Baghdad. Fatimid cells operated throughout Eastern Islam, grouped round highly trained missionaries, who were initiated in Egyptian schools and celebrated for the subtlety of their propaganda and, not unjustly, for their learning. Promotion matched with intellectual attainment, and authority rested on scholarly ability.

Persia was a receptive mission area, discontented with the 'Abbasids and, after 1040, with their allies, the Saljuqs. By a combination of cunning and ability to win over lower elements of the population – weavers, artisans, minor officials – the Isma'ilis gained strong points in various regions. They operated from mountain fortresses sustained by the local peasantry. Their assassins went out to waylay and murder influential enemies. The word 'assassin' came into Europe through the Crusaders. It was a nickname for adherents of the Isma'ili sect and derived from the belief that its agents must have been drugged on hashish – were *hashishiyun* – the explanation of their extraordinary courage.

One of their first victims, in 1092, was Nizamu'l-Mulk, the great minister to the Saljuq Sultans. Nizamu'l-Mulk was a staunch upholder of Saljuq power, which he tried to fashion in a manner he believed would benefit the Persian people. He was an implacable foe of the Isma'ilis, whom he dreaded as an insidious threat within the state against Islamic orthodoxy and the Saljuq Sultanate.

It is ironic that a legend first given currency at least as early as the thirteenth century should link Nizamu'l-Mulk with Hasan Sabbah, the foremost Isma'ili missionary and leader in Persia. As readers of Fitzgerald's Introduction to his translations of the Ruba'iyat will recall, Nizamu'l-Mulk and Hasan Sabbah are linked with Omar Khayyam in the story that they were all classmates under Muwaffaq, a great teacher in Nishapur, and made a compact that whoever of them achieved success in life first would help the others in their careers. Nizamu'l-Mulk attained rank and influence first and kept his bargain, satisfying Hasan by getting him a place in the government, and Khayyam by granting his not, it would appear, uncharacteristic wish to be afforded leisure for study. Sabbah was soon dissatisfied with his relatively low position, the less tolerable to him because of his jealousy of Nizamu'l-Mulk's proximity to the Sultan. An intrigue against his benefactors having failed, he left for Egypt and later returned to Persia to terrorize the régime Nizamu'l-Mulk so diligently and brilliantly served.

The story is improbable. Nizamu'l-Mulk was about thirty years older than the other two men, whose ages were likewise incompatible with their having been in the same class at school together. Moreover, there is nothing to suggest that Hasan Sabbah spent any of his boyhood in Nishapur, the home of the other two. Some have ascribed to him a Khurasanian ancestry, saying that his antecedents came from Tus in Khurasan, but he himself belonged to the city of Rayy, whose site is close to modern Tehran. The region of Rayy was quite distinct from Khurasan, lying well to the west of that province, and Hasan Sabbah went further west still for his training as an Isma'ili propagandist. When quite young he went to the schools of Egypt. After his return to Persia he obtained the stronghold of Alamut in the mountains north-west of Rayy. There, from 1090–91, he resided in his impregnable castle, furnishing its library, which Hulagu Khan caused to be destroyed in 1256, and directing the Isma'ili movement throughout Persia, the 'Order of the Assassins'.

It has been suggested, notably by Harold Bowen in a skilfully argued article in the *Journal* of the Royal Asiatic Society for October

1931, that the story may have been concocted by sympathizers of Hasan Sabbah in an attempt to show that his grievance against Nizamu'l-Mulk was justified because the latter had kept him subordinate when young. In bitterness he had been driven to go over to the Isma'ili Fatimid enemy in Egypt and later to lead their 'fifth column' in Persia – though in fact it was already there before he assumed its leadership – and finally encompass the death of his former friend. Concocted the story assuredly was, but Bowen argues the case that Nizamu'l-Mulk did in fact have two schoolfriends, one of them a poet, the other a theologian and jurist, whom he did help in after-life, while the story as it has reached posterity ignores these real classmates of the great minister, substituting the unlikely comrades, Hasan Sabbah and Omar Khayyam. Bowen's ingenious reconstruction of the identity of Nizamu'l-Mulk's genuine classmates is convincing, and his assertion that the trio of Khayyam–Nizamu'l-Mulk–Hasan Sabbah is spurious equally so.

A point which nobody seems to have noticed in this context is the telling phrase, quoted in our Introduction, from the early book on poetics called the *Kharidatu'l-Qasr* ('Virgin Pearl of the Palace'), in which Khayyam is described as 'proverbial' – his name, so to speak, a household word. Besides being relevant to the fact that a large number of ruba'is are attributed to him, this also seems to relate to Khayyam's inclusion in the legend of 'The Three Schoolfellows'. All three were famous men: Nizamu'l-Mulk was one of the greatest ministers in Persian history, Hasan Sabbah one of the most notorious heretics in Persian history, and Khayyam one of Persia's greatest astronomers and mathematicians, so that to link their names was natural. Sadiq Hedayat points out that they were all in one way or another upholders of the Persian way of life and values in the face of an alien régime. Though Nizamu'l-Mulk was this régime's faithful servitor, he was acting as a cushion between the Saljuq military rulers' exactions and oppression and the refinement and desire for fair dealing of his fellow countrymen. Hedayat's argument that Sabbah and Khayyam had in common their opposition to Islam and to hypocrisy does not bear close scrutiny and is due to his own preoccupations, but nonetheless his explanation, looked at in terms cooler than those in which he presents it, goes some way towards accounting for the three men's juxtaposition in the popular mind and a popular fable.

Though none of the sources we have used accuse Khayyam of the Isma'ili 'heresy', even when they calumniate him in other ways, he is mentioned in two Isma'ili books. Abdallah ibn Murtadh says in his *Falak ad-Dawwar* (as cited by Bernard Lewis in *The Origins of Isma'ilism*) that both Khayyam and Avicenna were secret adherents of the sect. Another and very important Isma'ili text, the *Haft Bab-i-Baba Sayyidna* ('The Seven Chapters of the Father Our Lord'), refers to Omar Khayyam in the section on the Eras and the date of the book's completion, but the context does not so much suggest that he was an Isma'ili as that his name had to be used in connection with the Jalali or Maliki Era which, as we have seen, he helped to calculate. So far as matters of religious affiliation are concerned, the bringing in of his name, with two others, seems neutral.

From what we know of Khayyam it does not appear likely that, for all their attention to science, he would have been attracted by Isma'ili extremists. He may have suspected them of using science for the wrong purpose, having harnessed it as they had to support their hierarchical and authoritarian management of a wide network of secret societies – not an organization it seems feasible for a man of Khayyam's temperament to have found sympathetic. He would not, surely, have brooked the abuse of learning, but it is impossible, after all, to be certain about his affiliations. He lived in difficult times long ago, and, in any event, eight and a half centuries later it cannot be easy to unravel associations that were of their very nature profoundly secret.

In the year 1809 Mountstuart Elphinstone was sent by the East India Company's government in India to the north-west, to find out all he could about Afghanistan. Near the Afghan border he sat and compiled a great deal of fascinating data on that country, receiving the reports of agents and the water-colour sketches of artists who delineated the different features and styles of dress of the Afghan people. When Elphinstone's *Account of the Kingdom of Caubul* was published in London in 1815, the text was illustrated by excellent coloured prints.

On p. 209 he described a libertine sect which flourished in the capital of Afghanistan, Kabul, and particularly attracted a dissolute element in the ruler's court. The leader of the sect was a certain Mulla Zakki, and Elphinstone says that its adherents were 'sometimes confounded with the Soofees'. They maintained that 'all prophets were impostors, and all revelation an invention. They seem very doubtful of the truth of a future state, and even of the being of a God.' Elphinstone continues:

Their tenets appear to be very ancient, and are precisely those of the old Persian poet Kheioom [sic], whose works exhibit such specimens of impiety, as probably were never equalled in any other language. Kheioom dwells particularly on the existence of evil, and taxes the Supreme Being with the introduction of it, in terms which can scarcely be believed. The Soofees have unaccountably pressed this writer into their service, they explain away some of his blasphemies by forced interpretations, and others they represent as innocent freedoms and reproaches, such as a lover may pour out against his beloved.

He goes on to say that the adherents of 'Moollah Zukke' are 'said to take the full advantage of their release from the fear of hell, and the awe of a Supreme Being, and to be the most dissolute and unprincipled profligates in the kingdom. Their opinions, nevertheless, are cherished in secret . . .'

Elphinstone's narrative cannot be regarded as unprejudiced, but it is interesting to note that he draws a distinction between 'Soofees' and outright libertines. His doubts about why Khayyam should have been drawn into the Sufis' service do not seem to arise from uncertainty about Khayyam's own position regarding Sufism, but from his belief that atheism must be totally alien to Sufism. Sufis for him were simply excessively devout worshippers of the 'Supreme Being', so that he could not account for their respect for a poet who denied such a Being's existence. He would be able neither to condone nor to comprehend the recourse of people tired of the fanatically imposed restrictions of a rigorous and legalistic religious code, to the sweet freedoms advocated and the humane witticisms pungently expressed in some of the ruba'is.

There is further evidence in works on certain amoral Indian sects for the involvement of Khayyam and his 'teaching' in various cults to be found on religion's wilder fringes. But none of these much later developments can be taken as a reliable gauge of Omar Khayyam's own position in relation to the life of the spirit. Life is lived very publicly in the East. As a result, though the heart is much talked of, men have learnt how to conceal what is really in it and, while verses might beguile a moment of leisure among friends and win applause for the poet's skill, they very rarely, as any student of Persian lyrical poetry knows, reveal precisely what the poet believed or did not believe.

'Thou shalt not make to thyself any graven image, nor the likeness of anything that is in the heaven above, or in the earth beneath, or in the waters under the earth.' The words of the Second Commandment reflect the Semitic view of the graphic arts, common to Jews and Arabs alike: no living creature was to be represented. This prohibition does not actually occur in the Koran, but one of the *hadith*, or traditions, makes the Prophet say that on the Day of Judgement artists will be confronted with their creations and challenged to bring them to life. Failing inevitably to do so, they will be consigned to hell-fire; they have usurped and abused the creative function of the Deity.

The art of book illustration certainly existed in Iran before the Arab conquest, though no examples have survived. We hear of wholesale burnings of books by the illiterate and fanatical victors, during which molten gold from the illuminations and pictures was observed trickling out of the fire. The possession of 'images' and illustrated books, if discovered, could cost the owners dear, as in the case of the great general Afshin, a Persian who served the Caliph well but whose services availed him nothing when he faced a charge of 'idolatry'. He was crucified alongside two other Persian patriots in 841, and this pitiful spectacle inspired an Arab poet to write:

Morning and evening they ride on slender steeds, brought out for them from the stables of the carpenters.
They stir not from their place, and yet the spectator might suppose them to be always on a journey.

But the Persians had a thousand-year tradition of royal portraiture and figural design, going back to the sculptures of Cyrus, Darius, and Xerxes at Pasargadae and Persepolis, and persisting strongly under the later dynasties of the Parthians and Sasanians. They accepted Islam when the Arabs conquered them in the middle of the seventh century, but they could never accept the Arabs' ultra-Puritan view of the arts. A certain restraint was, however, practised; large sculptures were no longer executed, but the tradition of illustrated books, dormant for a time, was gradually revived, the sinful pictures being tactfully concealed between the covers of volumes on library shelves. Even there, however, they were not always safe from the vandalism of fanatics, and many miniature paintings have come down to us with the figures defaced or obliterated.

The terrible conquests of the Mongols during the thirteenth century caused a further wholesale destruction of libraries and works of art of all kinds, and there is very little left to show us the state of painting in Iran in the preceding centuries. They swept in from the north-east through the populous and highly civilized province of Khurasan, leaving a wake of smoking ruins and unburied corpses. City after city fell. At Marv, a typical instance, over 700,000 of the inhabitants were massacred, and a few days later a Mongol detachment revisited the place to hunt out survivors, of whom they managed to catch and kill 5,000. Finally, in 1258, came the turn of Baghdad, the capital of Islam, and at that time probably the greatest city in the world. It too fell, and during the sack, which lasted a week, nearly a million of the inhabitants were slaughtered. 'Then there took place', says a contemporary historian, 'such wholesale slaughter and unrestrained looting and excessive torture and mutilation as it is hard to hear spoken of even generally; how think you then of its details? There happened things I like not to mention; therefore imagine what you will, but ask me not of the matter.'

But paradoxically enough the Mongol conquests sowed the seeds of classical Persian painting by opening up communications with China. During the fourteenth century, while the Mongol conquerors were absorbing the civilization of their subjects, there took place a remarkable fusion of Chinese and Byzantine elements with relics of native traditions of painting stretching back in some cases beyond the Arab conquest; but of these contributing factors the Chinese was by far the most potent and productive. Thus at the end of the century the true Persian style of painting was fully formed, as can be seen in a splendid manuscript of 1396, executed at Baghdad for a prince of the minor Mongol dynasty of the Jalayrids, and now preserved in the British Library (MS. Add. 18113).

But already the next wave of invasion from Central Asia was on its way; Timur (Tamerlane) and his Tartars repeated the dreadful sequence of slaughter and destruction, overrunning the whole of Iran, Baghdad, and the Ottoman dominions of Asia Minor. By the beginning of the fifteenth century, however, Timur's sons and other relatives – the Timurids – were established in the various cities and provinces of his empire, and some of them showed themselves by no means uncultured and unappreciative of the arts. The most notable among them at first was his grandson Iskandar Sultan, who combined a stormy political career with the exercise of an enlightened patronage. The artists who worked on the manuscripts he commissioned had probably been trained in the Jalayrid style of Baghdad, to which they brought additional refinement. After his fall in 1414 these artists seem to have transferred their services to Baysunghur Mirza, another grandson of Timur, under whose patronage the art attained even greater heights of imaginative treatment and technical perfection. He was governor of Herat under his father Shah Rukh, and established there an academy of book production in which more than forty artists and craftsmen – calligraphers, painters, illuminators, book-binders, and so on – were employed. His brother Ibrahim Sultan meanwhile presided over a simpler but bolder style of painting in the south-western centre of Shiraz.

The power of the Timurids was in decline towards the middle of the fifteenth century, and by 1455 the only territory left to them was Khurasan with its capital, Herat. The rest of Iran had come under the rule of the Turkman princes of the Black Sheep and White Sheep clans, who had manuscripts illustrated in the styles of both Herat and Shiraz, but who later evolved a recognizable court style of their own. Meanwhile at Herat the last great Timurid monarch, Sultan Husayn Mirza, held a brilliant court throughout his long reign (1468–1506), surrounded by eminent poets, historians, musicians, and painters, amongst whom was Bihzad, generally considered to be the greatest Persian painter of all. Under his influence the sometimes stiff and formal character of the earlier court painting was relaxed into a growing naturalism, though he always respected the basic canons of the art.

As the sixteenth century dawned, Persia was united under a Persian monarch for the first time for 850 years. A great national revival established the Safavid dynasty under Shah Isma'il, who claimed descent on one side from the Prophet, and on the other from the ancient royal house of the Sasanians. In painting he and his successor Tahmasp inherited the court styles of the Turkman and Timurid princes, which combined by about 1525 to produce paintings of greatly expanded scale and almost overpowering magnificence. The emphasis is on the splendour and elegance of court life, and some of the strength and virility of the best Timurid painting is lost.

By the middle of the century uncoloured drawings and separate paintings were becoming increasingly popular as patronage spread downwards from the court as a result of the settled condition of the country. Subjects were taken more and more from everyday life. It is from this phase, which lasted till the fall of the Safavid dynasty in 1722, that most of the illustrations in this book are taken. Omar Khayyam's quatrains often celebrate the joys of wine and dalliance, and such subjects are numerous in the later sixteenth and – even more – the seventeenth century. It will be clear from what has gone before that no Persian paintings of this kind (nor, indeed, of any other kind) have survived from the time of the poet himself, but those shown here illustrate admirably the spirit of many of the quatrains.

The earliest in date (p. 64) is perhaps the most brilliant of all, and full of robust humour. Sultan Muhammad was second only to Bihzad, and the leading court painter under the first two Safavid monarchs; he has here depicted every stage of intoxication in masterly style – even the angels on the roof are carousing! But drinking need not always be indulged in with such abandon, and on pp. 53 and 85 it is seen as an elegant pastime, while the paintings on pp. 54 and 87 represent its idyllic aspect. After wine, love; and Persian artists could depict all its phases from the first tentative advances (pp. 77 and 91) to the closest embrace (p. 113). The more intellectual and philosophical moods of the poet are aptly caught in the calligrapher on p.100, the young reader on p.41, and the learned discussions shown on pp.38, 59 and 82.

The leading figure in Persian painting between about 1590 and 1630, the period to which the great majority of these illustrations belong, was Riza (pp.54, 59, 85, 87, 97, 100, 107 and 113), who worked for Shah 'Abbas at his new capital of Isfahan, and whose style is a perfect evocation of the elegant decadence and languid hedonism of his period. These qualities are sometimes encountered in Persian poetry, and the drawings and paintings here reproduced may thus provide a visual commentary on the quatrains. They may also give a certain insight into the poet's mind. But the strongest justification for their presence here is that they are wholly delightful in themselves.

B. W. Robinson

LIST OF ILLUSTRATIONS

Numbers in *italic* indicate page reference

Frontispiece: The prince, with the philosopher and attendants in foreground. Safavid period/Isfahan style, *c.* 1600. Bibliothèque Nationale, Paris [Sup. pers. 985, f.2r.]; *38:* Five sufis seated at the foot of a tree near a stream discuss the virtues of mystical love. Safavid period/Isfahan style, *c.* 1590. Chester Beatty Library, Dublin [MS. 236 f.57r.]; *41:* A young man reading. Riza, after a lost original by Muhammadi of Herat. Safavid period/Isfahan style, *c.* 1630. British Museum, London [1920–9–17–0298 (3)]; *42:* Seated girl playing with her cat (inscribed 'Caesar's daughter'). Safavid period/Isfahan style, *c.* 1600. Bibliothèque Nationale, Paris [Arabe 6075, f.6]; *45:* A youth telling his father of his love. Attributed to Muhammad Qasim. Safavid period/Isfahan style, mid seventeenth century. Chester Beatty Library, Dublin [MS. 268 f.13v.]; *48:* Young man offering a cup. Probably by Sadiqi. Safavid period/Isfahan style, *c.* 1590. Bibliothèque Nationale, Paris [Pers. 1171, f.2]; *50:* Six figures in a landscape. Possibly by 'Ali Asghar. Safavid period/Isfahan style, *c.* 1590. Chester Beatty Library, Dublin [MS. 237 f.2r.]; *53:* Drinking party by night. Safavid period/Herat style, *c.* 1590–1600. Chester Beatty Library, Dublin [MS. 250 f.152v.]; *54:* Bird and scene of lovers with an attendant. Riza. Safavid period/Isfahan style, *c.* 1610–20. Seattle Art Museum (gift of Mrs Donald R. Frederick); *56:* Portrait of a young man. Possibly by Sadiqi. Safavid period/Isfahan style, *c.* 1600. Bibliothèque Nationale, Paris [Arabe 6076, f.15]; *59:* A prince in council. Riza. Safavid period/Isfahan style, *c.* 1590. Bibliothèque Nationale, Paris [Sup. pers. 1313, f.147]; *60:* In a pavilion adorned with a fresco, a seated prince receives a letter from a kneeling man. Safavid period/Isfahan style, *c.* 1590. Chester Beatty Library, Dublin [MS. 236 f.50r.]; *64:* Universal Drunkenness. Sultan Muhammad. Safavid period/Tabriz style, *c.* 1530 (The Cartier Hafiz). Courtesy of the Fogg Art Museum, Harvard University, Cambridge, Mass.; *66:* Youth in a pink turban. Signature of Mu'in Musawwir. Safavid period/Isfahan style, *c.* 1660. Collection of HRH Sadruddin Aga Khan [Ir. M 44]; *69:* Lady with a flower. Sadiqi. Safavid period/Isfahan style, *c.* 1580. Bibliothèque Nationale, Paris [Pers. 1171, f.32]; *70:* Young woman dancing with a scarf before a young man. Signature of Mirza Muhammad al-Hasan Khani. Safavid period/Isfahan style, *c.* 1630. Bodleian Library, Oxford [MS. Ouseley Add. 174 f.6r.]; *73:* A young man receives instructions from a shaikh. Possibly by 'Ali Asghar. Safavid period/Isfahan style, *c.* 1590. Chester Beatty Library, Dublin [MS. 237 f.1v.]; *74:* Lovers seated in a garden with an attendant. Attributed to Muhammad Qasim. Safavid period/Isfahan style, mid seventeenth century. Chester Beatty Library, Dublin [MS. 268 f.16r.]; *77:* An elegantly clad youth falls in love with a girl whom he meets, and who has drawn aside her veil. Safavid period/Isfahan style, *c.* 1600. Chester Beatty Library, Dublin [MS. 247 f.69v.]; *80:* Young man seated holding an apple and a wine cup. Style of Riza. Safavid period/Isfahan style, *c.* 1615–20. Chester Beatty Library, Dublin [MS. 246 f.1v.]; *82:* Two men converse in a rocky landscape. Safavid period/Isfahan style, *c.* 1625–50. Musée d'Art et d'Histoire, Geneva (Pozzi Bequest 79); *85:* Young man seated on a rock holding an apple and a wine cup. Riza. Safavid period/Isfahan style, *c.* 1615. Chester Beatty Library, Dublin [MS. 296 (i)]; *87:* Fête champêtre. Riza. Safavid period/Isfahan style, *c.* 1610–15. Keir Collection; *91:* Lovers. Muhammadi. Safavid period/Khurasan style, *c.* 1575. Museum of Fine Arts, Boston (Goloubew Collection) [Acc. No. 14.588]; *94:* The prince and the philosopher, with attendants. Safavid period/Isfahan style, *c.* 1600. Bibliothèque Nationale, Paris [Sup. pers. 985, f.1v.]; *97:* Youth in a crimson turban. Riza. Safavid period/Isfahan style, *c.* 1630. Chester Beatty Library, Dublin [MS. 260 (i)]; *98:* Two men, one a young prince, converse in a pavilion; two ladies sit on the terrace before them. Safavid period/Isfahan style, *c.* 1590. Chester Beatty Library, Dublin [MS. 236 f.143r.]; *100:* A calligrapher. Riza. Safavid period/Isfahan style, *c.* 1610–20. British Museum, London [1920–9–17–0271 (1)]; *104:* Young aristocrat and young dervish. Safavid period/Khurasan style, *c.* 1590. Collection of HRH Sadruddin Aga Khan [Ir. M 33]; *107:* Youth kneeling on one knee. Riza. Safavid period/Isfahan style, *c.* 1630. Chester Beatty Library, Dublin [MS. 260 (iii)]; *110:* A young warrior. Safavid period/Khurasan style, *c.* 1580. Bibliothèque Nationale, Paris [Arabe 6075, f.9]; *113:* Two lovers. Riza. Safavid period/Isfahan style, *c.* 1630. Metropolitan Museum of Art, New York (Francis M. Weld Fund, 1950).

To provide a complete bibliography of the very extensive literature on Omar Khayyam and the Ruba'iyat would be a major undertaking. In the small selection given below, one bibliographical work is included, while several of the titles contain fairly detailed bibliographies.

Arberry, A. J., *The Romance of the Rubaiyat*, London, 1959

Bosworth, C. E., *The Ghaznavids: Their Empire in Afghanistan and Eastern Iran, 944–1040*, Edinburgh, 1963

Boyle, J. A., 'Omar Khayyam: Astronomer, Mathematician and Poet', Bulletin of the John Rylands Library, Manchester, Vol. 52, no. 1, Autumn 1969

Browne, E. G., *Literary History of Persia*, four vols., Cambridge, 1951–6

Browne, E. G., *Revised Translation of the Chahar Maqala*, Cambridge and Leyden, 1921

Christensen, A., *Critical Studies in the Ruba'iyat of 'Umar-i-Khayyam*, Copenhagen, 1927

Dashti, 'Ali, *Dami ba Khayyam* ('A Moment with Khayyam'), Tehran, 1966 and 1969, translated into English by L. P. Elwell-Sutton as *In Search of Omar Khayyam*, London, 1971

Elphinstone, M., *An Account of the Kingdom of Caubul*, London, 1815

Heron-Allen, E., *The Ruba'iyat of Omar Khayyam* (a facsimile of the MSS in the Bodleian Library), Boston, 1898

Heron-Allen, E., *Edward Fitzgerald's Ruba'iyat of Omar Khayyam with Their Original Persian Sources*, London, 1899

Heron-Allen, E., *The Second Edition of Edward Fitzgerald's Ruba'iyat*, Duckworth, London, 1908

Hodgson Marshall, G. S., *Cambridge History of Iran*, Vol. V, Chap. 5

Huma'i, Jalalu'd-Din (ed.), *Tarabkhaneh* (Persian text), Tehran, 1342/1963

Kasir, D. S., *The Algebra of Omar Khayyam*, New York, 1951

Minorsky, V., 'The Earliest Collections of O. Khayyam' in *Yádnáme-ye-Jan Rypka*, Prague, 1967

Nicolas, J. B., *Les Quatrains de Khèyam*, Paris, 1897

Pagliaro, A., and Bausani, A., *Storia della letteratura persiana*, Milan, 1960

Potter, A. C., *A Bibliography of the Rubaiyat*, Ingpen and Grant, 1929

Rempis, C., *Beitrage zur Hayyam-forschung*, Leipzig, 1937

Rosen, F., *Ruba'iyat-i-Hakim 'Umar-i-Khayyam* (Persian text), Berlin, 1925

Ross, E. E., with Gibb, H. A. R., 'The Earliest Account of 'Umar Khayyam', Bulletin of the School of Oriental and African Studies, Vol. V, 3, 1929

Shafi', M. (ed.), *Tatimma Siwan' ul-Hikma* of 'Ali ibn. Zaid' ul-Baihaqi (Arabic text), Lahore, 1935

Shamsu'd-Din, Muhammad ibn Qais ar-Razi, *Al-Mu'jam fi ma'ayir ash'ar al-'Ajam* (Persian text), E. J. W. Gibb Memorial Series, Leyden and London, 1909

Terhune, A. M., *The Life of Edward Fitzgerald*, Oxford, 1947

Tirtha, Swami Govinda, *The Nectar of Grace; Omar Khayyam's Life and Works*, Allahabad, 1941

Whinfield, E. H., *The Quatrains of Omar Khayyam*, London, 1883 and 1901

Woepke, F., *L'Algèbre d'Omar AlKhayyami*, Paris, 1851